Love life & All the dots

Love life & All the dots

Deepak Verma

Srishti
PUBLISHERS & DISTRIBUTORS

Srishti Publishers & Distributors
Registered Office: N-16, C.R. Park
New Delhi – 110 019
Corporate Office: 212A, Peacock Lane
Shahpur Jat, New Delhi – 110 049
editorial@srishtipublishers.com

First published by Srishti Publishers & Distributors in 2012
Copyright © Deepak Verma, 2012

ALL MAJOR CHARACTERS IN THIS NOVEL ARE 100% FICTITIOUS
ANY RESEMBLANCE TO ANYONE LIVING, DEAD OR TO BE BORN
IS PURELY COINCIDENTAL

Typeset in AGaramond 12pt. by Suresh Kumar Sharma at Srishti

ISBN 9789380349626

I'm walking in your shadow ever since you went away.

And the clock on the wall really has not very much to say.

Oh, you left me bleeding

And left me needing—you

Acknowledgement

I am so glad that you are finally reading my story. It has been a dream for many years and the long and tiresome process in writing my first book immediately evaporates the moment I see my dream becomes a reality. Truly, it was difficult to sit for hours and push myself to write but I really enjoyed the journey.

To start with, there are many wonderful people around who have inspired and helped me over the years to fulfill my lifelong desire of writing a book. It's my privilege to acknowledge and thank all of them, and in particular,

My family-Mother, Brothers, Sisters, Brothers-in-law, sisters-in-law, Nephew and Nieces who have all stood by my side in all difficulties and inspired me to achieve my goal.

Niraj Sinha from Exhibitionsnow.com and Lipi Patel, for being my first reader, when the whole book was in just the form of a hand written manuscripts and believing in me that it could be translated into a book.

Raj, Pablo, Shashank, Safir, Sagar, Nishant, Neha- Amazing friends who painlessly read and re-read my manuscript every time and gave some honest feedback.

Asif, Naiyer, Priyanka, Priya, Periwal and Anand, Guddu, Mahto, Gaurav- Friends from the time I was growing up in a small city without any dream and who, made me believe to dream and make it a reality.

Venky Sir-Thank you very much for providing me the honest feedback. It means a lot to me.

I am also indebted to a number of authors whose, books I read and got inspiration from. Last but not the least the entire team of Srishti, who believe that my creation could be translated into a book and made me feel that I belongs to this group of people who want to share something to the outside world.

AND THE CLOCK ON THE WALL REALLY HAS NOT VERY MUCH TO SAY. OH, YOU LEFT ME BLEEDING AND LEFT ME NEEDING—YOU

"You sure, you are going?" shreya asked me.

"Yeah, am sure. I have to go". I replied and kept on packing my stuff.

"But you could go after your paper. I mean it's the last paper on Monday." She replied back.

"This is the most important semester and you are going just before the last paper." She continued.

"She is in trouble shreya. She needs me." I replied and look at the clock hanging silently on the wall.

"I will be back soon." I left in a hurry as I had to reach Howrah station in just an hour, before the only train to Ranchi could leave from the platform.

I had already called for a cab. I directed the cab driver to push the accelerator as fast as he could and moved towards the station.

The last call from Pia kept rushing to my mind. She was in absolute pain. Irrespective of what had happened in the world, she would never want me to leave my paper as she had seen me undergoing so much stress to reach to an institution of repute. I kept looking at my watch every passing second and with every movement of the needle I could sense a faster movement of my heart and soul. I wanted to reach the station way before time as I had not even booked a ticket.

"Please fast," I told the driver unmindful of the fact that he was trying very hard to keep pace in the horrifying traffic on the roads of Kolkata.

"Do you know any shorter route dada," I further poked him.

"No, this is the best route to go to the station." He replied and keeps on pushing the cab here and there keeping in mind the urgency of mine to reach the station.

I knew the train always leaves the station 10-15 minutes late but I had this suspicion that today it would leave exactly on time.

I saw the time. Twenty minutes to nine. It would leave at 21:05 hours.

"Fast dada, train chalo gache." I could see Howrah bridge from a distance and thus felt as if it would be soon that we will reach the station.

I reached exactly fifteen minutes before the schedule departure. I gave two hundred rupees to the driver and ran towards the platform. It would not have wise to go for the ticket as it would mean the departure of train. I rushed towards the train pushing a number of fellow passengers and vendors in the way and hopped onto a compartment. The train was almost full and I sat on a vacant position near the lavatory and waited for the conductor to come make a ticket for me in case the train has some vacant seats.

Last few months have not been really good for us. I had been observing some difficulties in the way Pia was living there. She had not been enjoying her stay as much as she used to. I had tried many times to know if everything alright but she never let her problems affect our relationship. She tried to control herself in front of me but I knew somewhere she had been struggling. I had stopped myself a fortnight ago when she hurriedly left her third semester examination in between and left for home. She just told me that her mother is not keeping well and she would return soon. She didn't say anything this time too but I knew there is something more serious then I had anticipated and she really needs me.

WHEN YOU SAY GOODBYE

I woke up by the sound of morning tea vendors and fellow passengers. I removed my blanket and looked outside the window. A new day had begun. I could see fellow passenger collecting their stuff and could sense that the station was about to come. I pulled back the blanket and tried to sleep some more when I heard someone saying that the train had reached Namkom station. I knew we would reach Ranchi in next fifteen minutes. I had not slept well, as I had not got a berth and had spent most of the night sitting in one posture on the seat meant for the conductor near the lavatory. I got a chance to sleep on one seat only when train reached Bokaro station as the passenger on that seat had got down there. The journey was not at all pleasant ,keeping in mind the chilly weather of December. I had forgotten to take any warm clothes with me in the urgency to catch the train and thus had kept on sitting overnight grappling with whatever that could save me from this cold. I forced myself out of the blanket and looked for my shoes which by then had moved in different direction in the midst of people grabbing their bags and other things. I stretched my body in what could be a way to provide much needed energy to my veins across the body which had frozen by sitting overnight in this freezer.

I got down at the Ranchi station and was welcomed by a flurry of cold wind coming across the station. It made me shudder from inside my already uncovered body. It actually helped my sleep deprived body in gaining the much needed consciousness. I got out of the station and took an auto-rickshaw and moved towards my home.

They had not expected me to come so early. They knew I had an exam on Monday and I would come once it is over. I reached home thirty minutes past six and knew that the door would be open as my father had been out for his morning walk. This has been his routine since long irrespective of the weather condition. I entered into the home to the utter surprise of my mother. She is anyway happy to see me home. I knew it's going to be really hard to convince my father why I had come in between the examination. I had to keep my answer ready before he could sense anything wrong. I went straight to my room and washed my face with water. I had been feeling quite sleepy and thus feeling a kind of heaviness. Had I tried to catch some sleep now I would not be able to meet her as we had planned to meet at the central market at nine in the morning.

I was getting myself ready to go when I saw my mother coming towards me with a cup of tea.

"You are going somewhere beta?" she asked and kept the cup on the table near me.

"Yes ma, I am going to meet someone." I replied and saw that my father had entered the door.

Before he asked anything I bowed down and touched his feet.

"You came today only. You had an exam on Monday na?" he asked the same question which I had anticipated

"Yeah, that has been postponed for a later date and thus I thought of coming earlier than scheduled. I replied hurriedly and sat on the bed to wear my shoes.

He didn't seem to be convinced with my answer as I had hardly looking at him but didn't ask anything.

"You are going somewhere?" He asked the moment he saw me tying my laces.

"Yeah dad, need to meet somebody. Can I take your scooter?" I asked and tried to move the topic further away.

He didn't say much and went towards the verandah for his morning paper.

I took the keys and silently moved out of the house.

I wanted to reach central market as early as possible even though I knew she would be coming around nine. I just could not engage myself in any other work and would rather wait for her at the market. I had always wait for her and I wanted to do the same this time too. It took me almost 5 minutes to start the scooter and soon drove towards the market. It was just ten minutes drive from my place and thus reached the central market half an hour before nine. This is one of the many advantages of living in a small city compared to a big city. It never takes more than a few minutes to reach any corner of the city. The shops were closed and very few people were there. The municipality van was trying to remove all the litter from the place to make it better for present day activities. I had made at least ten rounds of the entire shopping complex when it struck 8 on my watch. By then, even the stray dogs had started looking at me in suspicion.

The security guard kept a watchful eye on me from a distance. Their suspicions ended only when they saw Pia coming towards me.

"Hi Rahul" she said as soon as she reached and I saw her usual smile was missing.

"Hi honey, how are you? What happened?" I asked holding her both hands.

"Why did you seem terrified over the phone? Is everything fine?" I continued for a few seconds.

"No Rahul, I just came to say you goodbye," she said.

"What.......? Why......? What happened........?" I exclaimed in disbelief.

"What are you saying dear? Where are you going?" I continued again.

"Please do not ask, shona. I will not be able to tell you now. We might not meet again. I have to go" she replied and I could see her wet eyes.

"What happened honey? Please tell me," I was asking her like never before.

"I am going to Canada tonight and do not know when I will be back." she said.

"But why so sudden baba? Everything was fine till yesterday" I pleaded.

"Tell me what had happened that you are going abruptly leaving everything behind. Think about me honey. How could I live without you? I will not be able to live my life without you. Tell me what has happened that you have decided to leave everything behind and go there."

"I love you Rahul. I have never thought of my life without you.

But I have to go." She was saying and my heart was beating faster with every passing second.

"Think about it dear. Tell me at least what had happened. Perhaps I have some solution for it." I was trying to convince her.

"Think about the degree for which you have been working so hard. It hardly six months and you could see yourself out of this prestigious management college. You would become what you have always dreamt off." I was trying to give whatever reasons I had.

"I do not know Rahul. My family needs me. My dream is shattering in front of me but I am not in a position to hold it back."

She exclaimed as if she was hiding something.

"I love you, Pia. Tell me what happened. Perhaps we could overcome it in the same manner as we have been overcoming so many difficulties since the time we have met. Our love will conquer all the boundaries. I know dear, you are hiding something from me. Please do not do this."

"Promise me Rahul, you would continue doing what you have been doing so well. I am not in a position to tell you anything now. I have no idea whether I would be back but one thing is sure, I will never be able to forget the time that we have spent together. You will always remain as my first and last love." She said almost holding her tears on the edge of the eyes.

All my efforts to stop her seemed to be in vain. I could not make her tell me the reason why she was going to Canada, moreover when everything seemed all right a few days before. There was something very serious but I believe it was pointless to insist. However, one thing was for sure, I witnessing my world being crumbling down like a pack of cards.

Goodbye Rahul, I have to go now. I will miss you," she said as I saw tears rolling down her eyes.

I was frozen. I wanted to hold her but my hands were not moving. I was standing like a dead soul. Do not know when she disappeared from my eyes, however, I kept on looking at her.

THE DAYS AFTER...

Whatever just had happened to me, it seemed like a dreadful dream. Whatever it may be, I wanted it to remain a distant dream. I do not know how long I kept sitting there, on the pavement when a flurry of noises brought my brain into the realm of reality. I saw many shops had opened or in the process of opening for the day. I felt quite terrible. My head was hurting and I felt a kind of dryness around my neck. I was thirsty. I went to a nearby shop and bought a bottle of mineral water. I gulped down the whole bottle in one breadth. I felt better. Everything came rushing back to my mind. I recollected everything that had happened to me in last one hour. With every thought, my head felt heavier. With that heavy head, I rushed back home.

"Where had you gone so early in the morning?" My father asked me as soon as I entered the drawing room folding his morning newspaper.

"Went to see a friend dad." I replied quite irritably and sat on the sofa.

I was fiddling with the pages of a political magazine and seemed almost lost in thought when he asked again.

"Any problem son? I saw you in the morning. You seemed to be in a hurry." He said and sat close to me. Perhaps he had sensed some problems.

He had never been so caring. He must have thought something else I believe. We had never sat so close ever. I wanted to hold him tightly and cry. I don't know what stopped me from showing my emotion. Perhaps I had never done that before.

"No problem dad." I said and went towards my room.

I lay on the bed and tried hard to sleep. My head was still hurting and I felt a kind of uneasiness. I pulled the blanket all over me and tried hard to get some sleep. I kept on changing sides in between and tried not to remember her but all my effort s seemed to be gone in vain.

I went to the kitchen. Got out a bottle of water, gulped down the whole bottle again, and moved back to my room.

I was in trouble. I did try to get some sleep many times, but could not get any. I kept on moving from one place to another. My anxiety level had been increasing with every passing second. I found no solace around and thus decided to call her.

With that heavy heart I went towards the phone, dialed her number only to disconnect it without any ring.

A week had passed since she had gone and the pain of her absence was haunting me with every passing second. I had been in great pain. It had never happened to me before. The worst part was, I had none before me whom I could have found some solace. I was desperately missing my friends with whom I had shared all my ups and down, but found none before me. The vacation was ending and I had to go back to Kolkata, moreover, this time she would not accompany me. The mere thought of her not been around was enough for me not to return to Kolkata.

Nothing would be same there. The day will not start with talking to her and it will not end without meeting her. Many thoughts were rushing down my mind. At one point I thought of not going back to Kolkata. The last thing that I had anticipated or foreseen was living in Kolkata without her. I was trying to hold myself. I thought I would be alright and forced myself to believe that and assure myself that things would be fine in a few days but things only got worse. My parents were quite anxious as to why I was not returning to Kolkata. They were quite apprehensive seeing that I had not been behaving well. They asked several times what had happened but every time I told them that I was alright and would return to Kolkata soon. I overstayed for one more week in anticipation that time would heal my pain and I would be fine to restart my course but the same feeling attacked the moment I tried to think about going back to my course. However, life had to go on and I had to move with it. I had garnered whatever energy was left in me and finally decided to return. I had promised her to continue what I have been doing so well and thus in next few days caught the train back to Kolkata. My father has come to see me off this time. The excitement of returning to Kolkata was almost gone and it took me a great effort to board the train. As soon as train started to move away from the station I felt a kind of jumping off it and return home. I do not know what stopped me from doing that. for so many days I have been trying to forget what had happened to me but the more I try to forget the more it come back to my senses. I had been still in disbelief that she has gone and would not return. I had been recollecting every second of my life with her.

THE FIRST ENCOUNTER!!

Physics lab would always retain a special place in my life. I would always remain indebted to the professor who taught me how to see a Vernier scale. If it were not for this scale, I would have never had the opportunity to talk to Pia. I really do not know if that was the case, but because of the scale, she came to me and we started talking. Perhaps we were destined to meet. I had been doing my major in mathematics after failing to qualify in any of the engineering entrance exam even after appearing it for second times. Being the youngest of four siblings, I had been pampered a lot and in all probability would get the better things in life then the other three. I had been sent to a better school than my brother and sisters as my father could not afford the same luxury for all of us. He was working in the account department of state electricity board and thus had limited resources. He wanted at least one of his sons to become an engineer and thus sent me to a better center of learning as well as provided me all sorts of facilities. I, on the other hand, was unaware of all these happenings. I have no idea as what made my father think that I could be able to fulfill his dream. I had not been a consistent performer in terms of educational achievement. I had almost nothing to prove that I could be a better bet. Leave apart academics, I believe, I never had any aspiration as in what I really wanted to become in life. As expected I could not qualify in any of the engineering entrance exam and in all probability I never imagined what my father would have undergone knowing the fact that none of his sons could become an engineer ever. In that sense, I had absolutely no inkling of the fact as in where I had been moving and what I wanted to achieve. Having failed to qualify in any of the engineering colleges, I had no options left except to go for a regular graduation.

Fortunately, on account of some good percentage in mathematics I got a decent college to pursue my major in it. It was an all boy's college and had a separate girl's wing which was separated by a lake known as Ranchi Lake. This lake was very neat and calm, and many kinds of water birds perch over it. It was situated exactly in between the two wings of the college and thus provides a great view from the rooftop of the college. The facilities of boating were also available and thus it offers great opportunities for people who wanted to have some leisure time out of the college especially for those who had a companion. Most of the time, the lake is flocks by the couple from far flung areas out of the preying eyes of their parents. We had a common administrative building in our campus and thus girls were allowed to enter into our campus for administrative works. That was the only good thing as far as our college is concerned. Pia was in the girl's wing and was doing her major in chemistry. For the entire first year I could hardly find more than ten students attending the class. The campus used to be deserted most of the time. Not only the mathematics department but all other departments had the same attendance. One day I even checked the number of admission in the mathematics department and was surprised to see the list of sixty students. I had hardly met with ten peoples in the entire year. Thus, nothing had changed in the last one year except the fact that I had been quite regular in the campus. That way I could enjoy more time away from home. Or in other word, I had to face my father less after the disastrous performance of mine in engineering. By that time, we had reduced our interaction as far as academics was concerned.

In my second year, two of the most significant developments had happened in the history of our college. The first one was the introduction of Bio-Technology course. We were the first ones in Ranchi to introduce the course. It had gained importance around the country by then and thus brought a lot of curiosity among the students who had failed to qualify in the medical entrance examination. The introduction of Bio-Technology course in our college brought a new lease of life in the campus as it brought with it some of the trendiest girls in the campus. Most of them were those, who somehow missed the qualifying percentage in medical entrance.

Introduction of Bio-Technology had brought some relief for them as it saved them from doing the mundane degree course. Unlike today, we had fewer options. The second significant development

17

was common practical classes for boy's as well as girl's wing. Both the development spread in the campus like wild fire. The same place, which looks like desert some time back, is blooming with the arrival of fresh faces. I witnessed a significant increase in the number of attendance. Most of them used to come to check out the girls. Soon the corridor which connect bio-technology department was abuzz with the movement. Almost every boy used to pass the corridor at least once to have a glimpse of those few beautiful girls. People started to find excuses to go towards the corridor.

The scene was like, if you are in the company of a girl, you will be loved by all and many boys would like to be friend with you. Obviously, the boys from the bio-technolgy would like to protect them from the preying eyes of everyone. They behave as if they own them and glances other in such a way that they were just a piece of shit paper. Girls, on the other hand, were enjoying all the attention. Who said, being in the minority is a disadvantage. Go and ask those girls. They were just the most sought after and that is mainly because they were in the minority.

Attendance, used to be abysmally low in a normal class but it had to be hundred percent at the practical class. That is the power of girls. The practical class used to be absolutely packed. The reason was obvious. That actually forced the college authority to make groups for practical as it was very difficult to manage such a large group at one go. The one who, was lucky enough, got the company of girls, other had to abide with the system. I was very lucky to found four girls in my group and thus become an overnight hero in the mathematics class. Pia was also in my batch.

There were thirty people in a group. It was a mix of students across all streams. There were twelve groups in all. Each group gets three hours of practical class in a day twice a week.

Therefore, we had two days or more precisely six hours in a week, where we could get a chance to mingle with those nice girls. It makes no difference to those who gets no girl in its group. But who cares, this is the time when no one really bother about others.

Every week we would be looking forward for the practical classes. A couple of session had already happened and I had very little interaction with any of the girls. On the third class, I was standing at my place and doing some work with the vernier scale when I saw a bespectacled girl standing next to the professor chair holding the vernier scale in hand. I was standing very close to where our professor sat. After a few minutes waiting there when she did not find the professor, I saw her coming towards me. Like a studious boy I kept on fiddling with the scale as if I was going to change Einstein's theory of relativity. I could see her come closer and stand beside me.

"Hi, I am Pia." She said quite confidently.

"Hey, I am Rahul" I was nervous. Probably for the first time I had an interaction with a girl "Could you tell me how to use a vernier scale." She asked the next moment.

"Actually I could not understand it yesterday when the professor was telling." She continues.

19

"Yeah sure." I said and immediately took the scale from her hand.

For the next five minutes I meticulously explained her how to see the scale. She heard it patiently and when she understands it clearly, moved back to her place leaving behind a small thank you. As she was going back, I thanked my professor, whom, a day before I had asked the same thing. It would be so embarrassing had I did not know the answer. Perhaps, I had scored in our first meeting.

LIFE BLOSSOMS ON THE CAMPUS!!!

Introduction of common practical classes brought with it a sort of miracle in the campus. Those two days of practical class in a week were absolute fun. The atmosphere of the college had gone for an absolute makeover. It would not be wrong to say that arrival of girls in the campus has completely metamorphosed the ambience of the college. The same guys, who were absolute disaster in terms of behavior, had become more cautious. There was a new enthusiasm in the air. It had made everyone more responsible. The same guys who at one point of time had never watched what dress they were wearing to come to the campus had now become quite fashionable. The attendance had increased to almost cent percent. The same campus which a few days before looked deserted had now filled with a lot of activities. Was it the power of girls or the scarcity of it that we had faced over the years? The question would remain unanswered to me. However, one thing is sure, we were having one of the best days of our college life and no one had any complain. More so, it was mainly a boy's college which never had the privilege of having a girl in the campus.

I have seen, in the last one and half years, there were absolutely no interaction among students of different departments. Low attendance might be a reason but I have been observing that introduction of Bio-Tech as a subject has actually increased the cross-departments interaction.

Moreover, the increase in attendance had forced the college authority to introduce common practical classes, which ultimately increased the cross-departments interactions many a fold.

That was quite amazing and good for the college. This new enthusiasm not only restricted to academics only but also spread to other functions of the college.

During our trial for selection of inter-college annual badminton tournament I met Ravi. We were selected from our college as a pair for the doubles event of the tournament. He is from the commerce department with which we never had any interaction. That was mainly because by the time we reached for our classes, they used to finish their and had returned. Morning shift were only for the commerce department. On our several encounter during the training session I came to know him better. He was very passionate about two things. One, he wanted to complete his accounts honors and do management in finance from an institute of repute and move for investmentbanking and second, he was very passionate about badminton and would never lose an opportunity to play the game. I believe, for the first time I had met with a guy who had a plan in life and he was working ahead as per the plan. The more I met with him, the more I use to be impressed with his sincerity and dedication to work. Soon we became good friends and moreover, won the double event quite convincingly. We were the only students to have won a major title in inter-college tournament. This had given us an edge over others. We had become popular in the campus.

Next few meetings with Pia always ended with formal greetings.

We never had any lengthy conversation. As soon as the practical class gets over, we all dispersed to our respective departments. I was too shy to even go close to a girl and start a conversation. I would always want to talk and interact with them but never had that kind of authority to go and initiate a conversation. One fine day while having tea with Ravi at the college canteen, I saw her coming towards our table.

Hiii, no class?" she asked gently.

No, class is on but as usual we are out." I replied quite convincingly.

"Oh, so bunking classes. Even I had come for some work and thought of having a cup of tea." She smiled and said casually.

C'mon, join us. By the way this is Ravi. He is from accounts honors." I said as I saw him uncomfortably glancing at her.

"Yeah, I know him. You both won that inter-college badminton together." She replied and I know what had this win done to our

23

reputation.

We kept silent for a few seconds. ·

So, you normally do not go for the classes." She asked as I took a sip.

But you are regulars in practical's class." She said immediately Yeah," I just replied and thought how I could tell you why we are so regular during practical's Sitting with a girl in canteen was not a common sight in our college. I saw a lot of eyes staring at us. She seemed absolutely unfazed by of all this. We were more uncomfortable probably because we never had this privilege. We hurriedly ended the session and moved out of the canteen.

So, you are coming for tomorrow practical," she asked as we were leaving Yeah," I said and I saw her going out of the campus with a gentle smile.

Since that day, I made sure to go to her and meet her. I do not know how but from then onwards, we made sure to talk once after every practical class. I started to go to meet her even if we did not have our practical. We had become good friends. Ravi, Pia and I often went across the road to the nearby café and used to spend a lot of times. During this period, I came to know her well. She was the second of the three siblings. Her elder brother was in the final year of engineering and little sister was in her 10 standard. She was born in Canada as her father was in Toronto and was a professor of Physics in Toronto University. Her family had moved to India when she was in seventh standard. Her father though had moved back to

Canada last year. She was very close to her dad and thus, used to miss him a lot. I, on the other hand, was very happy with this new development in my life. I had been learning a lot with this troika of friends i.e Ravi, Pia and I. Out of three, I was the novice. I had little knowledge about the outside world. I had no ambition. I did not know what I would do after my graduation. I always felt a bit like an outsider when Pia and Ravi talked about their career plans. But one thing was certain, in their company I had started to learn of many new developments across the world. I was trying to focus more on my career now. They had filled in me, a sense of self awareness. I had started to take things seriously. I knew that I had made friends who could be a positive influence in my life. With every passing day, our bonding was becoming stronger. We had started to meet at least once every day and on every meeting I was the one who was learning something special. On one such meeting, while having our usual tea at the café, I heard them talking about the Common Admission Test for Management.

Did you see the advertisement for CAT in the newspaper?" Ravi asked Pia that day Yup, its on 20 November this year and the last date of application is 15 Oct." she replied.

CAT…..What is that?' I asked quite mysteriously.

It's a common test for the best management college in India and that is Indian Institute of Management." Ravi promptly replied.

I had heard of IIT. I had also heard of IIM but did not know how to go about it.

Yes, if you want to study at the best management college in India, you have to clear CAT." Pia elaborate as I put my cup after having the last sip.

We had our second year final semester exam in a couple of week's time. I knew nothing except the fact that I had to clear all my semester to become a graduate.

So, you people are going for CAT this year?" I asked quite mysteriously.

Nope, we are not eligible to apply as only candidates who have passed or in final year of graduation could appear for the test." She said and looked at Ravi.

We could appear for it, but that would only to gain an experience. We would not be able to take admission this year." Ravi clarified and I heard him quite intently.

Moreover, it is better to appear for it when you have a good preparation." He continues.

I believe, we should start our preparation as early as possible, so that we could be exam prepared before next year." He was telling and I was getting more intense with the conversation

By that time, having an MBA degree would have opened a plethora of opportunities. Other than engineering and medical professional, people with an MBA degree were the most sought after. The economic reforms that the Government of INDIA has done in 1991, was giving fruit.

With the opening of economy, more and more foreign companies were entering into the country and this has made an MBA even more popular. The companies across the globe were looking for people having degree in management education. I returned home that evening and the conversation that we had kept on revolving around me. I wanted to know more about it.

Next morning while sitting with Ravi at the college canteen I asked him if we could go for the preparation of CAT.

"You know what, the whole night I kept on thinking about CAT." I said Ravi.

"Really, Pia and I had decided to join a coaching class for it." He said and I raised my head in bewilderment.

You didn't ask me." I complained.

"I would have asked you anyway before we go for it." He gave an explanation.

"Bloody, you forgot, I had the one who introduced you to Pia." I joked and he smiles casually.

"Hahaha…don't worry we would be going for the coaching class together." He smiled.

"You must have decided about the coaching class as well." I poked him further.

"You don't need to. We have just one good institute here. AMS." HE HAD DONE ALL THE HOMEWORK!

"And we would be going there today only to know about the courses and timings." He said and stood to go outside.

I followed him.

Next moment we were heading towards the main road leading to AMS on his Bajaj Priya scooter. He was the selected few to have a scooter. AMS was at the heart of the city and was based on the 8 floor or on the topmost floor of the biggest commercial space available in town. We had investigated every details about the course. The duration of the course, timing of classes as we had to attend our college too, the fee for one year classroom coaching and question related to faculty and infrastructure. We also verified all the details with the students already enrolled for one year coaching class and are undergoing the training. We came out of the building only when we had satisfied with the standard of AMS as the only and leading coaching institute for MBA. We had decided to go for it and within a week took admission for what I believe was the start of an exciting journey of our lives.

THE JOURNEY BEGINS!!!

$2$1st October, 2000.

The first day at AMS.

Pia, Ravi and I reached AMS sharp at 8'o clock as has been told to us. We had been given the slot from 8 am to 10 am. Two hours of classes everyday and then we are free for the day. The moment we entered into the reception, we saw a tall and handsome guy with a beautiful girl standing by the side of reception. They were discussing about CAT. There was no one at the reception and thus we stood there and waiting for someone to come and tell us what to do.

"You all are new joinees?" that tall boy asked us as we were waiting there.

"Yeah, we joined today. Don't know where to go and thus waiting for the receptionist." Ravi replied and I saw them came closer to us.

Don't worry, we also joined today." He replied and burst into laughter which I could not understand.

I saw him fiddling with his fingers. He was more than 6 feet tall and quite thin. A light tikka adorned his forehead. Those big eyes inside a well suited pair of glass seemed to be looking for something and I could easily see the gentle smile on his face.

Hi, I am Priyesh." He moved his hand and we shook hands.

Helo, I am Rahul. She is Pia.

An...d I am Ravi" he said before I could introduced him.

"She is Ruchika." Preyesh said pointing towards that beautiful girl.

We had talked for five minutes when I saw someone calling us from behind.

"Hey, you all for CAT 2001 batch?" He said and moved towards us.

"Yeah," we said in unison.

"Hi, I am Anand. Your coordinator for the year." He said and we all shook hands.

He called us inside a room where I saw something like more than twenty students already sitting. They were all like us. We sat on remaining seats farthest from the white board. That was the beginning of our session. We first had half an hour introductory speech by the owner, Mr Bajaj where he spoke about what it takes to become an MBA. He gave an overview of the management education and how to go about it. We had been introduced by the faculties and staffs and where we had to go for our requirement. First day had ended in all these introductory session. We had met with a few students though and were quite impressed with them. While coming out of the institute, we saw Priyesh and Ruchika standing along side a small café and drinking coke.

"Hey, how was the session?" Priyesh asked the moment we reached there.

"Good, nothing excellent." Ravi responded before I started.

"Oh, you people want to have coke?" He asked.

"No, Thank you." Ravi replied straight

Bloody, at least ask us. I thought.

"No thanks buddy! We are just getting late for our college." I had to obliged Ravi.

First few days went on knowing about place, faculties and people. Gradually, session started to gain pace. Every other day, we had to face some kind of mock test and we had been judged on the basis of marks that we had been obtaining. That was the tool to identify our intellectual capacity and on the basis of that they used to differentiate the level of brain we possess. They use to do this practice with all the batches to make different groups based on intellect. People with same level of intellect were kept in one group and they had been coached accordingly.

They used to make groups as per the following level which we later on understood as they did not want to hurt anybody sentiments. There were three groups. People who were certain to clear the test, people with potential and could clear with some coaching and third were rest of the folks who could not be included in the first two. I would not like to bracket those into any name. We were included in the second group.

It has been over a month in AMS and in last one month, other than usual stuffs, we had made a few friends. Other than Priyesh and Ruchika, we had been quite regulars with Asad and Namit.

We had always seen them together. It would not be wrong to say that they were like a couple.

Every morning they used to come together and took the corner seats farther from the white board. On a few interactions with them, we found them quite an interesting people. Asad was more of a reclusive and used to keep to himself. On the other hand, Namit was an extrovert. It was Priyesh who introduced us to them and since then we have been in constant touch. We used to have a little conversation after the class before we all left for the day. On several occasion we used to go to the nearby Café Kavvy and used to have nice conversation over a cup of tea. This has become a regular features and in every occasion I was the one who came out as a learned man. On most occasion, our conversation were concentrated on the preparation for CAT and how to go about it. I was particularly impressed with Asad. A well built, small height guy with amazing sense of latest fashion. He always wear a well creased shirt with matching trousers. A well suited spectacle adores his face. In first impression he could easily bowled anyone out with his sense of understanding with different topics. He speaks with a great accent and that had added to his charm. I had never met with anyone with such a great knowledge of English literature. On several meetings with him, I came to know about his background. He belongs to a well educated muslim family. His forefathers had worked closely with the British Empire and thus the tradition was well carried forward in genes. His father was a senior public prosecutor and was serving with the district civil court. Namit, on the other hand was more of a carefree sorts of guy. He belongs to a middle class family with middle class upbringing. He was an extrovert and never hesitated to initiate a dialogue with anyone. We were caught in many awkward situation with his this attitude. He loves to watch hindi movies especially of Devanand. He had seen all of his movies as far as I know. He had an average educational background and thus had limited understanding. I was really amazed with his exuberance and boundless energy. In every adverse condition he would always come up with a smiling face. I do not know how he could do that with such an ease. He had a beautiful girl friend and thus he used to disappear as soon as class got over. Initially we were quite curious to know where he goes the moment class gets over. In a few days he introduced her to us. Her name was Ria. He was the only one in our group who had a girl friend, thus in the matters of heart he used to speak quite convincingly and we had no other option but to listen him. After all, he had experience something which we always wanted to but had little courage to propose someone.

Six months had passed and we had become a strong team. We used to share a strong bond among us. We had our own world and we were happy to be in the group. One fine day, while having our regular class we were introduced to Rishi. He had joined in our batch. The syllabus had already been half done and we were quite surprised to know about it. In first look, he seemed to be a few years older than us which is confirmed on our conversation with him. He was a short, fair and bulky guy. On every occasion we found that he kept to himself and did not like to talk to others. As soon as the class got over, he packed his stuff and disappeared from there. I had hardly seen him smiling and on most occasions he seemed to be silent. I thought as he had joined late and hardly knew anyone, thus he will take some time to acclimatize with the situation but after having been there for a month he remained the same. I found in myself an amazing curiosity to know about him. One day, while browsing a business magazine in the library, I found him coming towards the library. He went straight to the newspaper section and started to read one.

I deliberately went towards him and started to grapple with the newspapers.

"Hi," I said and started the conversation.

"Hello," he said and keeps reading newspaper.

"Hey, I am Rahul. "You have joined recently?" I asked him as I found nothing else to ask.

I wanted to have a conversation with him.

Yeah, I joined last month. Actually I took the decision to appear for CAT late." He replied and kept silent.

"So how did you find it. You have almost missed half the syllabus." I continued.

"You must be finding it tough now."

"Yeah a bit. But I am trying hard to catch up with whatever I have missed." He reasoned.

Oh, that great, tell me if you require any help. I have been regulars in the class from start. I offer my help.

Yeah sure, whenever I require I will ask you. Thank you." He said and involved himself in reading.

I tried not to disturb him further and went towards my seat.

From then onwards, we used to have regular conversation, though mostly related to books and subjects.

Gradually, we started to have more interaction and I introduced him to all the members of our group. Soon he started to come out with us for a cup of tea at our so called meeting point.

"So why did you join so late." I asked him one day while sitting at the library.

"Well…..",he stopped for a moment.

"Actually, I never wanted to do MBA." He said and stopped in the middle.

"Then why?"

"Hmmmn…you know Rahul, I had a flourishing business of medicines."

"But….."

"But what?" I asked curiously.

"Hmmn…but it all has been ruined," he said in a distress tone.

"Oh….sad"

"After graduating in Pharma, I had started one medicine shop. Within few weeks the shop started to earn profit. I opened another one and it all had been going on great.

But some wrong business moves has ruined everything. I was trapped in heavy debt and went into depression. I could not able to do anything for almost one and half years when my family had saved me from going into dump. They supported me and made me realize that everything is not lost and I should think of something else. Thus I started to think of doing an MBA." He said in one breadth and stopped.

I patiently heard him and was really very sad to know all about this.

"I am really sorry Rishi. You had really done your part. Perhaps that was not your destiny. There must be something better are ahead in your life." I tried to console him.

But I know how hard it is to loose something you really love especially if you have work so hard to made it. I could understand his pain but could not do anything except offering some consolation.

THE FIGHT FOR A BETTER TOMORROW!!!

It had been more than six months that we had joined AMS. In last six months, other than the usual classes, I had made some nice friends. We had a group. A group with different sorts of individual, different aspirations level, different likings but one objective and that was to make something out of this ordinary life. In our quest for attaining this objective, we were ready to do every possible thing. For me everything was like a dream. Since the time, Pia had come into my life, I had been observing in me a kind of new zeal. I had been trying to focus on my life. I had become quite regular in classes and had also developed a kind of hunger to learn new things.

Whatever might be the reason, but I had been observing some positive changes in me. I had been accepting whatever was coming up my way. A few months back, I had limited thinking and had absolutely nothing to do and now I had been struggling to find time to do my usual stuff.

Every other day, I found something new and would try to be the master of it. I had been learning a lot in their company and soon my brain started to work in the right direction. I had been picking up things from different people and was trying to do better on them.

I used to spend some more time with Ravi and used to learn from him different tricks of data analysis as he was perfect on it. We usually go onto the roof of our institute after the class and discuss it for hours. Out of us, Ravi and Pia were absolutely focused on the job. They had gradually started to avoid usual meeting session and would in all probability like to spend time in library. I on the other hand would want to be with them as in that case I was able to gather some inputs from them and secondly would get more time to be with Pia. By that time, I had developed a kind of affinity towards her and would like to spend time with her. She had no inkling of this affinity I believe. The usual morning class session was stretched up to late evening as the date for common admission test was approaching. Gradually, our usual meeting hours started to depreciate and moreover, for whatever time we met, we ended up discussing about the CAT and about keeping the stress level down.

"Are you coming to Ruchika's place?' Asad called me one morning.

"Yes, Ravi is coming to pick me up and we will both proceeds towards her home." I replied softly.

"Gr8!! Namit and I are also leaving soon. What about Priyesh and

Pia?" He asked abruptly.

"Don't know about Priyesh, but Pia must be reaching now. Priyesh anyway will reach there. After all it is Ruchika's birthday." I replied in excitement unknowing the fact that it would not go down well with him.

By that time, Asad had a strong liking for her. On the other hand, Priyesh and Ruchika seemed to have more liking for each other although they were not dating. It is probably because both of them were joined the institute together and thus had good chemistry.

We would be getting this get together after a long time, moreover, on a special occasion like this. It would probably be an ideal way to come out of the four walls of our home which by then had become our playground and probably forget about the exam for some time. It would probably give us some respite from the hectic lives and would unwind us for more hectic days to come. The moment we entered into her house, I saw Pia sitting along side Ruchika and Priyesh as usual muttering some stupid jokes of his. We greeted her and handed her over a bouquet which Ravi had specially brought for her. Soon her mother brought for us tea and some snacks to eat.

"Hello aunty." We greeted her and sat on the sofa.

"Hello beta, how have you all been doing." She asked softly and sat beside Pia.

"We all are good aunty. Just preparing for the exam." Ravi responded and we all took our cup of tea.

"Cmon aunty, only Ravi is preparing. We are only waiting for the exam." Priyesh jumped on with his senseless humour and we all know it would be to tease him. Since the time we had met, it seemed they were just not jelling well. Both never lost a chance to instigate other. Ravi never liked the extravagant way of his living and thus would want to be as far away from him as possible. Priyesh on the other hand, have not changed even an inch. He had never been serious about the exams and would in all probability know that he had to anyway look after his family business.

"Shut up!! Only you are waiting for the exam. We all are preparing." Ruchika intervene to protect our integrity.

Before anyone could speak further, someone rang the bell at the door.

Just a second, let me check. Aunty stood and went up to check.

Hello aunty," we heard the sound of Asad, Namit and Rishi.

Hello beta, please come in." she said soon they all enter and greeted Ruchika for her birthday.

You people took so long to come." I asked them the moment they arrived.

Asad must have been shopping for Ruchika." Priyesh exclaimed from behind and I could see his mysterious smile.

Bloody he just can not keep his mouth shut.

We all took it in light vain and soon all of us burst into full of laughter. Its been ages that we had been together like this and thus we were having one of the best time. We had forgotten about the impending exams and relishing the moment. Soon we were joined by

Ruchika's dad and her sisters. She is the oldest of three sisters. Her father was working with the custom and had posted in Patna. He had specially come for her birthday. Soon we all celebrated her birthday with usual cake cutting followed by a sumptuous lunch which her mom had specially cooked for us.

So what have you brought for her?" I asked Asad the moment we had our lunch.

Now please you don't start." He tried to be calm.

Its ok. I was just teasing you." I said and moved towards Rishi.

He was as usual quite silent over the time.

Hey buddy, how have you been? How is your preparation going? I asked the moment I reached there.

Gr8!!! Its been good so far. Don't know what going to happen but am really working hard." He exclaimed.

Don't worry, things would be fine." It is just a matter of three months now. You will see everything would be perfect and we all would be smiling at the end." I tried to sooth his nerves although I was also quite anxious by that time thinking of the prospects of impending exams.

Next few hours went by in a zippy when we all decided to return home. End to an exciting day full of fun and frolic.

The D-day was fast approaching and the pressure for the exam was building up. The classes were over and everybody was engaged on doing last minute revising. The usual meeting hours were absolutely non-existent though we used to have regular conversation over the phone but that generally about the impending exam and its preparation. I, though, keep on talking to Pia almost every day. I feel a great relief while talking to her after a hectic day of preparation. By that time, I had developed a great urge to speak to her or meeting her. My day would not be complete without dialing her number for once or sometime more then once. I started to find excuses to call her. She on the other hand politely says that I should concentrate more on the job at hand.

THE DAY WHEN EVERYTHING MATTERS!!!

We had a frenetic last fortnight or so. Quite predictably, it all began with last minute preparation and ended with the apprehension that if the question would be coming from the chapter that we had left. Asad was the one more superstitious kind of a guy. He would always come up something which would make you believe that whatever you have prepared over the years would not going to be enough.

"Did you know it is rumour that the pattern of the question paper has changed this year and they are going to put more emphasis on the reasoning part." He called me one midnight out of the blue.

"I really do not know from where you have been receiving such things but who cares. We have to go for the exam with the preparation that we have done. I do not think such things matter now." I replied quite mildly.

"Yaar, as the examination approaching, I have been feeling a kind

43

of anxiety." He said quite seriously.

"Don't think that much into it. Just relax and enjoy your time." I tried to calm him.

"Just concentrate on the basics and forget what's going to come on the examination." I reason him and make him comfortable.

"Now please put down the phone and relax a bit", I told him.

The date of the exam was fast approaching and we all had been doing the last minute reversing.

Ravi and I used to study together and would learn from each other strong point. It would not be wrong to say that we were competing with each other as who would solve the paper first and who would get more marks. He would be scoring more in data interpretation and I would defeat him in logical reasoning. We had planned to solve at least one full set till a day before the exam in last fifteen day. This way we would be able to know where we have come in terms of solving the problem and what last minute preparation require for it. We have set the timing as it will be going to be in the examination hall.

For the first time in my life, I was actually very happy to appear in an examination. It's been long since I have felt this way without my anxiety choking the life out of me. I had been more confident than the last time I had appeared for the exam. It had been a long time and I have learnt that if you have worked really hard to get something you would feel happy and confident that things would come out well for you. The same is happening with me. I had been working day and night for this moment. It is said half the battle is won if you are happy in doing the thing you want to and I have done exactly the same. I was filled with a great sense of excitement.

Looking at the way Ravi preparing for the exam had filled a new zeal in me. I keep on practicing set over set and would sometime did not sleep at all. I was really not thinking of what others are doing but keeping in mind that I had not been receiving any phone calls from my friends, I knew that they had been busy with the preparation as well.

Finally, the day had arrived. The CAT examination was going to be conducted across the country on the next day. The day had arrived for which we had been waiting for so long. I had been preparing to leave for Jamshedpur as we had our center there when my phone rang.

"Hey, what's up? How have you been?" I heard the voice of Pia from other end.

"Hey, great!! I am really good. Tell me how are things with you?"

"It's been great so far just a little apprehensive for tomorrow. I do not know what's going to happen." She was a little scared at the prospect of tomorrow's exam.

"C'mon, do not worry. I know how well you have been preparing for this day. Just relax and enjoy these moments." I calmly said.

"Do not know yaar, it's really getting to me now."

Everything would be fine. Just keep your cool and you would be really going to do well.

Hmmn, I hope so." She said and we disconnected the phone and promised to meet before the exam at the center.

It was a complete turn of fate for me. Some years back, it used to be the situation for me. I used to ask people about what was going to happen. In some instances, I was not at all interested to go for the test. I used to think different ways and excuses which could save me appe aring for the exam and avoid the post result embarrassment. I knew it was all because I was never exa prepared. I never had the courage to face any kind of exam. This had been a turn of fate for me.

People are asking me and talking to me for the upcoming exam. They thought about me and found me one to give them courage and motivation to go for the exam. For the first time I was not afraid. I knew I have the enough firepower to not only sustain the pressure but also to come out victoriously. It has been a long journey and has been filled with many difficulties and struggle. I had been really worked hard to come where I had been standing.

I reached the examination center one hour before the schedule start time. Asad, Namit and Priyesh were with me. We sat under a tree on the sprawling compound of the school. It was magnificent. I was looking for Pia and other group members. I saw Pia sitting at a distance with a book in hand. She had been accompanied by her mother.

"Hey, you are here." We greeted her mother and asked her.

"Yeah, great to see you all. I am really nervous." She said

Soon Ruchika and other group members joined us and we pledge to do everything that is possible and in our hand and would come out victoriously.

I entered into the classroom and sat on the designated area. I looked around me. People were already seated and I saw invigilators entered into the classroom with bundle of brown envelope in their hand. I knew it would be the question paper and answer sheet. I took a long breadth and pledged that this is the day I had been waiting for a long time and I have to do well. Next two hours passed like a bullet train zipped passed the station.

Phew!!! The exam is over. I had done well. The months of preparation and hard work had been sealed in just two hours. The fate had been sealed in the answer sheet. The moods post exam were the evidence of years of hard work that people have undergone. I saw the faces of people coming out of the center. Some had still in the flow of exams and I could hear the post exam discussion. Some looked tense while some clueless as what had happened. I found my group waiting outside and went towards them.

"Hey, how was the paper." Ravi asked me the moment I reached.

"Yeah, good, I think I have done well." I replied softly.

"Great, I feel I could have done better." He would never let his true self come out.

Asad looked a bit tense while namit and Priyesh were as usual in the mood of some fun. They were the least bother about all these hype surrounding the exam and post exam postmortem. I looked at Pia and her face told me everything. I knew she had done well but still apprehensive about the outcome. Ruchika were as usual smiling and I didn't not feel that I should ask her how she had done in the exam.

Well the exam was over and it was the time for some celebration. We had a good time while coming back to Ranchi.

A TRIP TO REMEMBER

"Bloody, where the hell are you? Are you on for the trip?" Asad shouted over phone.

"Which trip? Where are we going?" I enquired, as I had no idea as in which trip he was mentioning.

"Now, don't tell me you have no idea. Everyone knows it. We all are going," he replied.

"But, who all are going?" I examined again.

"Don't worry, Pia is coming with us," he smiled sensing as if I am asking about her.

"Oh no, I did not mean that," I retorted however he sensed it right.

"Now c'mon, be a man. Get out of the den and reach the institute in an hour," he replied and kept down the phone.

"Gosh, how am not I aware of it," I paused for a second.

In a state of bewilderment, I removed my blanket and hopped onto the floor. I had only returned in the morning from an overnight journey and thus, making up for the lost sleep.

It took me nothing more than half an hour to reach institute. This is one thing I really like about small town. It hardly takes a few minutes to reach anywhere unlike big cities where it takes hours to commute from one place to other. Thus, it takes almost no time for me to be ready and reach the institute.

"Man, u didn't tell me where we are going.' I quizzed Asad as soon as I reached the institute.

"Boy, look at the excitement. Do not worry soon you will come to know about the whole programme."

"Hmn, great. However, who else is going? I asked again, sensing I would be able to get the answer I wanted to know.

"Oho my lover boy, where were you man?" Priyesh jumped into the conversation in his indelible style when I saw Ruchika and Priyesh joined us.

"I had gone to my sis's place. How you guys are doing?" I asked them.

"Great, someone was looking for you.' He winked at me and I knew what he was trying to say.

However, what he did not know is I was in constant touch with Pia all these days. But, she never mentioned about us planning a trip. Perhaps, she was not planning to go. However, by that time, I was addicted to have her presence around me. I wanted her to be on my side every time. I wanted to tell her how much I love her and thus, looking for a better opportunity. It would be great if she join us in the tour, as I would get enough time to be with her and know if she has the same feelings for me. Mere thought of her not joining us on the trip was enough to douse all the excitement. I wanted to know if she is on for the program.

The common admission test for IIM was over. God knows what was in store for all of us.

Gradually, we were trying to come in terms of our daily routine. There were no late night studies. The regular classes were over and we had some time before we could start afresh for rest of the examinations. The New Year was fast approaching and it was the time for celebration. It was an ideal time for those, who knew they would certainly cross the first barrier of the toughest management examination in the world, to regroup and refresh themselves for the next big challenge as well as for those, too, who somehow did not manage to do well but was keen to rejuvenate themselves for the rest of the examination. It was tough too, to persuade them to come for the celebration as they somehow not in the best frame of mind. I have seen so many times how difficult it is to motivate oneself when in spite of the best effort, you just not able to perform at the D-day. The fear of not making it to the elite list of selected students is enough to shackles the confidence especially when the future is at stack at the outcome of the event. That fear was writ large on many faces. Especially after post exam postmortem when a silly mistakes cost us a few marks. I failed to understand the logic behind this postmortem. Once the exam is over, you cannot change the answer however silly the mistake was. On serious thought, I came to know that most of the people who do this activity are those who had some doubts about their selection. They are the ones who are serious contender for the elite list of selected candidates. I believe there are three types of candidates. First of them is the one who are sure to get into that list. Second is the one who is most likely to get the seat on sheer hard work and lastly the one who always knew that this is not his cup of tea. If you belong to the second category, it is going to be sleepless night until the declaration of the result. They would always thought about the answer they could have made and would always remain in the dilemma. I was one of them in the same category. Actually, I never belong to the first category. I never had the courage to look at the result, as I always knew the outcome. My brother always used to do this for me and he used to get disappointed to see my name missing. For the first time in my life, I was eagerly waiting for the result. I had no idea about the outcome.

It had been over eight months that we had joined this institute and all these months we never had an opportunity to enjoy as a group. On most occasions, we had competed with one another. We had been fighting hard to outclass another in the race of life. People were divided in a number of smaller groups. It would be a perfect opportunity to break that jinks and come to know about one another. The time was perfect too. At one hand, we were relaxed after the most difficult examination in the world (as people say) and on the other hand we were on the verge of saluting the year passing by and welcoming the dawn of a new year. A year filled with many expectations and promises. Thanks to our institute in providing us, the much needed energizer. We had a lengthy deliberation over the choice of location. After looking at all the possible location, we decided in favour of Panch Gagh falls mainly because of its proximity from Ranchi. The falls is located on the Ranchi-Chakradharpur highway, approximately 8 KM from the Khunti district. It has newly developed as a tourist destination and considers being one of the beautiful falls in the country. We had never been to the place. Naturally, we wanted to explore it. We had been together for last one year and during those times a number of couples and to be couples had formed. Obviously, we had been looking forward to having some exciting time. In fact, those days unlike big cities, we hardly get time to be together. We generally do not get such freedom. Thus, we do not want to waste an opportunity like this where we would get quality time to be with the person, we like, moreover away from the preying eyes of our parents. I was not an exception. I wanted to make sure, if Pia is coming for the trip or not.

Asad, though, told at the beginning that she is on for the program. However, knowing her well, I had my doubts about her coming for the trip. Soon I found her in the library and asked her if she is on for the trip.

"Hey, are you coming for the trip tomorrow?" I asked her.

"You would miss me if I do not come." She smiled.

"Yes, I will." I said as I do not want to waste this opportunity. She looks amazing when she teases me. God, I would do anything to have a moment like this.

"Don't worry; I would not let you miss me". She said and a cute smile appeared on her face It was just so beautiful.

Next morning I reached the institute sharp at 7 o'clock to board the bus for the trip. Soon Namit, Asad, Priyesh and Ruchika joined me. Gradually, more people joined in and bus started to fill. However, there was no sign of Pia. She must have reached by now, as we had to leave by 8 o'clock. My anxiety kept increasing after every passing second. I just cannot imagine going out without her. It is almost 8 when I decided to call at her place and enquire what has happened.

We went to the nearby PCO and dialed her number to find that she has just left her house and must be reaching by now. That was enough to calm down my anxiety. While returning to the bus, I found her standing near the bus and smiling. Perhaps she came to know about my calling at her. Bloody, sometimes friends do more than what you expect them to do, especially matter as sensitive as this. Anyway, it always helps.

"So, you thought I am not coming." She asked as soon as I reached there.

I had no answer except to smile and sit on the bus. Soon we started moving towards what, I believe, an exciting journey of my life.

They say time flies when you are having fun. That is exactly what happened with us. We did not realize how two hours passed by. The atmosphere in the bus was electric. We were singing and dancing as if we have come out of some shell after many days of struggle. After moving for almost two hours on the highway which connects Chaibasa, a small town on the south chotanagpur district of Jharkhand from Ranchi, we reached a place called Khunti. On further 6 km from Khunti the bus took a right turn to the service lane and soon we were heading towards a deep forest. It was a narrow lane and in all probability no two buses could cross each other, I believe. In next 20 mins we reached a secluded place inside the forest when bus stopped. We had reached our destination. We could easily sense the beauty we are going to witness. On further walking for 10 mins along the bushes and concrete road, we finally reached to a place surrounded by mountains and forest.

"Wow!!! It's incredible." Asad screamed the moment we reached.

It is really amazing. I had never seen such a beautiful place ever. I saw five parallel waterfalls running down from the mountain and meeting with a rivulet flowing across the plains which ultimately met with the river Swarnrekha which I later found out. I thought for a second about the source of this water but soon left the ideas and ran towards the waterfalls as many had already jumped onto the pool. I could hear nothing except the sound of water hitting the mountains and the screams of people enjoying the experience of bath underneath the gushing water. I hopped onto a small platue and touch the waterfalls from a distance. I spread my wings inhaling the fresh, chill air, still intoxicated by the beauty of this place. The moment this intoxication removed, my brain looked around the place to search for Pia. For sometimes the beauty of this place kept my mind off her.

From a distance I saw Pia sitting beside the rivulet with her feet inside the water. She had worn a green kurti and a black jeans. The gentle winds were making her hairs to roll over her cheeks and she constantly trying to keep it away. She was not wearing the specs which she usually does. That has been replaced by contact lens I suppose and that makes him absolutely gorgeous. I thought it was a perfect opportunity to go near her, bent on my knees, hold her hand and say that Pia I love you very much. Will you be mine forever, ever?

With that feeling, I went towards her. The moment I reached there, all those thoughts just disappeared from my mind as soon as she lifted her head and smiled at me keeping the hairs gently behind her ears. I just could not muster the courage to say all these. I wanted to keep on looking at her gentle smile. For a few moments, I kept on standing in front of her when she raised her hand and helped me sit beside her. I, being a gentleman, sat a few feet away from her. Everything that I had desired to say remain inside me for the moment.

"What are you doing here alone?" I asked.

It looks so beautiful from here. Look at the waterfalls strutting down from the mountains, hitting onto the earth and flowing through this rivulet. She said in excitement.

"Yeah, it's just amazing. I had just seen a place like this in movies"

I replied casually.

We kept silent for a minute. In the silence, the sound of water flowing through the rivulet was crystal clear. I saw her playing with the sand from her feet. The same thoughts of proposing her kept revolving around me. I could easily hear the palpation of my heart which was beating many times faster than the normal.

"You know, when my father was here, we used to go out every now and then." She said the moment I clear my throat to speak up.

"But, since the time he left for Canada, we hardly go out." She said and I could easily read her disappointment.

"You love your dad na?" I said casually.

I love my family. my father, my mom, my sister and......." She stops in between and my heart started beating faster.

Would she was about to say my name." I lost in thought.

"And what Pia?" I poked her further to know the answer.

"And my brother." She murmur and all my excitement gone down Bloody, she had almost made my heart burst. Soon I returned from my dream.

"Where is your brother? You have never told me about him." I asked her as she had never mention about her brother since the time we had met.

"He is in USA. He hardly speaks with us nowadays." She said and I could easily see her pain.

I didn't try to ask her further and changed the topic.

I thought of asking her as in what she thinks of me when I saw Asad jump from behind and join us.

"Hey, you people are here. Everyone was asking about you two," he said.

"Yeah, we were about to come there," I replied looking at him distressfully. "Fucker !you had to come now only." I thought

"It's a great place na" Asad asked again.

"Yeah, come on, let's join them, I said and stand up as I knew he would not let us sit there and we went towards the group which already had engaged in some form of activities.

Its umpteen times that I wanted to ask her about what she thinks of me and if she likes me but every times somehow things did not work out.

. . . .

As soon as we reached there, we saw everyone asking Namit to sing a song. He generously accepted the invitation. Bloody, he was always on the lookout for such occasion. I knew he would sing something from Devanand movies and I would have to applaud on his stupid singing prowess. He tried to clear his throat before singing like a professional singer and there he is…..

Hai apna dil toh awara,

Na jane kis pe aayega

I saw Pia make her way to the group and sit on a small plateau beside Richa. I made myself comfortable a few feet away from her and at a position from where I could see her from an angle. Soon I flew myself in the realms of imagination, keeping myself in the Devanand shoes and singing the same song for my lady love when a sudden burst of clapping broke my slumber and brought me back to the reality. I smiled and joined myself in applauding him.

Gradually more people joined in. The intensity had increased and almost everyone had to do some form of activities before we gather again for lunch. I was very impressed with Rishi. We all knew he used to play the guitar very well but we came to know how well he sings too. Like a true professional he started to sing,

Purani jeans aur guitar

Mohalle ki who chat aur mere yaar"

I had no knowledge about the intricacies of music but listening to him did give me a feeling of originality. His guitar perfectly matched with each and every word of the song.

Time had been passing quite well. Soon it was the turn for Pia to do some activities. I became more intuitive. Will she sing and if she sings, which song? She did nothing and politely refused.

The number was moving anti clockwise and I knew after two more people it would be my turn to do something. My brain started working on what I would do when my turns come. I could find nothing as I had never involve in any form of activities before. I thought I would also refuse but somewhere I wanted to do something like what Rishi did before. It would have been perfect to impress her. for the first time, I cursed myself for not knowing to play any of the instrument. I was involved in this thought when someone called me as its my turn now. In a hurry I said I would sing. Singing is the easiest thing to do, I believe, as even if I would not sing well, none would have complained. Now the question is, which song am I going to sing now? I had little interest in music and thus knew very few songs moreover 2-3 lines only. Soon I found out something I had heard while coming here in the morning and here I go......

Na tum hame jane,

na hum tumhe jane

Magar lagta hai kyu aisa,

Mera humdum mil gaya......

I could see Pia looking at me. She must be puzzled to know that I could even sing and thus many of my friends. I think, I had sing for the first time in front of so many people. Anyway, I did well and had been applauded highly.

I was the last one in the circle and thus we all move towards the lunch packets. It was the time to take much needed energizer.

"Kya baat hai boss." Priyesh exclaimed as soon as we took our lunch packets.

"Tum gana bhi gate ho. Aaj pata chala. Pia would be very impressed." He continues.

"Fucker, she is just behind you." I thought as I saw her coming towards us.

"Hey, you sing very well." She said as soon as she reached.

"Thanks" I said as I saw the mischievous smile on Priyesh face It was already 3o'clock when the owner of our coaching institute, Mr Bajaj joined us with his wife and a one year old son. He had come separately. We could not spare him as well and as a punishment for joining us late, he had to sing a song for all of us. He did not disappoint us and politely obliged.

Next few hours passed like a rocket. Like all good things, it also has to come to an end. With a heavy heart, but fresh mind, we returned towards our bus. As soon as I boarded the bus, I saw Pia sitting on the window seat of the second raw. The seat next to her was vacant. Namit and Asad were standing behind and rest of all had already taken their seat.

Someone has kept a seat for you." Namit said as soon as I reached there.

I did not pay heed to his comment or I better thought to ignore it and sat beside her.

The bus had already filled and had started to move. Being the month of December, the sun had disappeared early and darkness was engulfing. The atmosphere was filled with cold and light breeze. It was very cold inside. I saw Pia pulled a shawl from her bag and gently wrapped around her. The bus was gradually moving passed the bushes and concrete road and soon reached to the highway. The breeze becomes bolder. There was a silence inside the bus, probably because of the after effects of full days of enjoyment. The slow sound of songs from 80's movies was making the ambience inside the bus absolutely romantic. Pia was looking towards the window and I was sitting beside her almost a few inches away when suddenly.

Namit tried to squeezed him on our 2 by 2 seat and moved me further close to her thus remove whatever distance I had from Pia.

Hey, what happen." I asked abruptly.

He just smiled and I knew why he did so.

I turned my head towards her and she gave me a cute smile keeping her hair back of the ears.

I keep on adjusting my body to make her sit comfortably. I had never been so close to her. I tried to keep myself on that upright position but like all human being could not keep it longer. I had to move my hand across the seat above her shoulder. I saw her still smiling perhaps wondering what a stupid I am. I was freezed like an ice. I saw my heart beating faster again and sweating appears on my forehead on that chilly weather. I somehow gather my composure and kept my hand across her shoulders. The left torso of mine almost touching her right torso and I felt some rise in temperature. The bus was moving faster and the occasional bumps on the road made the distance between us even closer. I saw Namit deep in slumber.

I saw her moving her hand up and kept it on my thigh. I lower my left hand a bit and hold her almost taking her in my arms. She gently kept her head on my shoulders and soon I had the girl of my dream in my arms. I could easily feel her heartbeat which was going at a great pace. I took a long breadth probably to relax a bit. I inhaled the freshness of her cologne and was almost mesmerized.

I could feel her breath. It has happened to me for the first time ever in my life. That feminine touch. I was on cloud number nine. The ambience was perfect. Those romantic songs had made it ever better. On those feelings, I don't know when I slept only to get up at the voice of conductor. We had reached our base. I saw everyone had just woken up from the slumber and moving out of the bus. I saw Pia raised her head gently leaving some strands of her hair on my shirt. She just smiled and I did not speak either. We got down to the bus and moved towards our home. I looked at my shoulder. I could still feel her presence. I could still feel her breadth. Those few moments would always remain the best ever moments of my life.

I FINALLY PROPOSE......

My innumerable attempts to convey my feeling had failed. It had been more than six months that I had been trying to convey her how much I love her. On some occasion, I came close in expressing my thoughts to her but somehow it did not happen.

By that time my love for her had spread wide and far. It is not as if I fear of rejection but the moment I go towards her, the moment I see her, I forget everything. I could not stop myself and let myself get immersed in her cute smile and demeanor. I could not think of anything beyond her. I really do not know what stopped me from expressing my feelings to her.

"Did you tell her?" Ravi asked me one day as we were sitting on the rooftop of our institute building.

"No, I could not muster the courage to tell her." I replied in a very serious tone.

"I do not know what stops me from doing this." I continued.

He remained silent for some time.

"You know what, I feel she loves you." He said and move towards the edge.

"She is a girl. She would not initiate. We live in this society. As far as I know, a woman would never initiate." He tried to tell me logically.

It was so like him.

I know. Bloody I tried several times but could not utter those three simple words." I said quite irritably.

"What would happen if you tell her? She might say no. Atleast you would come to know that na.

Look at you; I have been observing you for many days. You do not seem like the person you used to be. You have forgotten everything. You do not spend that much time with us as you used to be. You have been struggling with yourself. You might feel bad for some times, if she rejects you but at least, you would come to know the truth. And suppose if she accepts you, what would happen than." He tried to explain to me.

"I would die if she says that she loves me." I exclaimed.

"You would die anyway, so be a man and just tell her." He said and winked at me.

"Day after tomorrow, we are going to Kolkata for our exam. She will also come and I believe this is the best chance that you could express your feelings for her." He said and we came down to move for home.

21st February, 2002, on a windy evening we boarded a train to Kolkata. Ruchika, Namit, Priyesh, Asad, Ravi and I were in the same compartment. Pia had not come with us. She was in a different compartment and her father accompanied her. We had met at the station for some time. I had met with her father for the first time. She seemed to be a caring man. I could not get a chance to talk to her much. Like today, those days' parents used to be a little apprehensive in sending the girl alone to a different city. We were living in a closed society. In our first meeting, I knew that her father was quite protective towards her. Soon we took his leave with the promise that we would stay in the same hotel and moved towards our coach. It was our first visit to the city. Among us, only Priyesh had visited the city. His family had a business there.

Obviously, he became our guide though I had a doubt that he would do anything keeping his track record in mind.

"He does not remember what he does last night. How could he remembers a city he had visited a few months back." I paused and took my seat.

It was an overnight journey thus, we decided to have our dinner and take a good night sleep.

We had our examination the next day.

"I had been trying to get a sleep but the same thoughts were revolving around me. I would not be able to get a chance to talk to her as her father was with her. By that time, I had become quite restless. I had no other work but to think about her. My day would not be completed until I talk to her twice daily if we could not meet. I had to tell her.

On reaching Kolkata, we again assembled at the railway station. As planned Priyesh take the initiative and directed us to take the taxi and move towards Chowrangi, a lane in the central Kolkata. It is also called Esplanade as we know once we reach there. He had become our leader.

We took a hotel and decided to meet on breakfast at the restaurant nearby. Asad, and Namit were in a room. Ravi joined me while Pia and her father were in a double room. Ruchika had to content with a single room all alone. Priyesh did not stayed with us as he went to his uncle house. We met at the breakfast and lunch table but I could not get a chance to talk to her as on both occasion her father was also present. She did come to Ruchika room but again for a brief moment. We went for some sight seeing in the evening and decided to return soon as we had our exam the next day. On reaching hotel around 8 PM, Asad, Ravi, Namit and I had a round table discussion. We neither discuss about the political instability in the country nor the constant infiltration of militants from across the border. We discussed about how could I be get a chance to tell Pia how much I love her. Though it was a bigger problem for me, I believe.

After an hour of brainstorming, we concluded that as I had not been able to speak to her, I should mail her my feelings and wait

for her to revert on the same. I had been warned by the three that
if I will not write to her, they will not talk to me forever. I had two
options either to speak to her and save my friendship or lose both. I
decided for the first.

Soon after dinner we went to the nearby cyber café on the opposite
lane. Namit sat on the key board. He wanted to write for me. We
stood around him like we had to crack some important puzzle. Soon
they were writing the script of my love story.

Dear Pia,

*This is I on your silver screen. I know you would be surprised to see this mail
of mine. I had always wanted to tell you personally but on every occasion I could
not had the courage to tell you. Since the time I met you, my life had been on a roll.
You have been a guiding force for me. You have taught me what life is all about.
I have learnt to live. I had no ambition, no direction and no goal but everything
changes the moment you came into my life. We became good friends and we have
been enjoying many good times. For some time I have developed some feelings for
you. In all honesty, I have to say that I like your company and I want to take
this relationship into a new level. I like you very much. I will wait for your reply
and remember we are good friends and we will be a good friend whatever your
reply would be.*

Yours

Rahul

Before I could read it again, Namit had pressed the send button. Bloody, sometimes friends do more than what they have been told to do. Anyway, I had finally proposed her though not in an usual manner. There were no flowers and I had not sit on my knees and neither holds her hand as has been shown in the movie. I had sent my proposal through a new medium and I am thankful to the person who had invented email.

WHEN SHE SAYS.....SHE LOVE ME NOT

It is said that time flies when you least expect it to be. Who knows it better than me? The moment Namit hit the sent button; I prayed that the night would not end. I prayed that the system get crashed and mail could not be sent. I prayed for all the possibilities, which could save this mail to reach to her. However, once you throw the arrow, it would not come back. I have done exactly that and I would wait for the consequences. I was the only person who could not react to any situation while coming back to the hotel. I did not know what had happened to me but the mere thought of her not accepting to my proposal was enough to freeze me like the ice. I did try to hide my emotion but friends actually become more intelligent in matters related to heart.

Your love for Pia must have reached by now to her mailbox." Priyesh teased me while coming back to hotel.

"Once the mailbox opens, it would jump into her heart and that will be the beginning of another love story." He continued.

"You fuckers, I am so scared and you people making fun of me." I cursed them.

"I do not know how I could believe you guys and did that." I continued.

"You morons, how could I face her once she sees it." I cursed myself.

"It happens. You have proposed a girl for first time na." Priyesh exclaimed.

"Yeah, and I do not want to be slapped for that." I stopped him in between.

"C'mon, everything will be fine. You have honestly told her your feelings. Now wait for her reply." Ravi tried to control things in his usual style.

"You are unnecessarily scared. I have done the same things. Now look at me, I have the girl I always wanted." Namit told his experience.

"You will see, once she read it, she would first try to ignore you.

When you would go near her, she would not react at all as if she had not read it. She would try to attract your attention and show a little nakhras." He explained as a master.

"But, you do not react much. Let her come to you and say." He continued.

"Idiots, it's not like any fucking hindi movie. It's a real life." I stopped him.

"Now, I will have to face her and tell her honestly once she sees the message." I said and threw myself on the bed.

Priyesh did not return to his uncle's house and stayed with us. We went on talking about the mail and its consequences once she checks her mail. Do not know when we fell asleep.

Next morning we got up late. We had our examination on the second half, thus we had enough time. I skipped my breakfast and went straight to my examination center. We had our return ticket the same evening. I was trying to avoid her even though I knew she would not be able to check her mail. I knew she would only be able to check her mailbox on reaching Ranchi. Next morning we had to assemble in the institute for the birthday celebration of Richa. I had a feeling that by that time she would be able to check her mail. We assembled at the GEL complex market which by than had become our meeting point. It was bang opposite our institute and had some nice restaurants. We went to our favorite Kavvy restaurant and café, which we often visited in a group. We wanted to give a surprise to Richa on her birthday. Ruchika had been given the responsibility to bring her a little late as we would be able to arrange everything by the time they come. We had already booked our place and ordered the cake. As soon as she entered the café, the air was filled with the music,

Happy birthday to you

Happy birthday, dear Richa

Happy birthday to you,

"Oh my god, thank you very much. Thanks a ton guys." She exclaimed in excitement and we went to congratulate her.

"How did you people do that? You all had returned this morning only." She was still in the excitement.

"Anything for you mam." Priyesh jumped immediately.

"Bloody, he never leaves a moment to comment on such occasion." I thought and looked at Pia.

She smiled at me and I thought that she had not checked her mail yet. We sat and ordered our food.

"Thank you guys, this is the best birthday I ever had." Richa was still in awe.

"And thank you for my present. Its very beautiful." She continued.

"Priyesh had specially selected it for you." Sometime Ravi become so unlike him.

He does not leave a chance to embarrass him. They both really loved each other.

We went home after lunch. Since I had not slept well in last three days, thus I went straight to my room and slept till someone woke me up,

"Oye, you have a phone call." My sister told me as soon as I woke up.

I saw the time. It was 5 o'clock in the evening. Time for Pia to call me. She does it almost every day.

Shit, what would happen if she had read the mail. I thought and went towards the receiver.

"Hello." I said.

"Hi man, sleeping? What happened to your love story? Asad shouted from the other end.

"Oh, its you. I thought….." I stopped in between

"Oh, you thought it was her." he completed the sentence

"Yeah, I thought probably she had read it and called me." I replied.

"Don't worry, she would reply soon." He said.

"She would call me only when you disconnect the phone." I said irritatingly.

"Oh, I am sorry. I forgot you had some important phone lined up." He tried to say emotionally.

"Fuck you, just hang up now." I would call you once I receive a call from her. I said and disconnected the phone.

I kept on waiting for her call.

One hour passed. Two hour passed. I did not receive a call. I knew something was wrong. She must have read the mail. I dialed her number many times but disconnected before it rang. I did not go anywhere and waited for her call but it did not come. My anxiety level increased many fold.

Next morning I reached institute half an hour before. I had

already informed Ravi to come early as he lives nearby. While sitting in the library with him, I saw Pia coming towards us. I could sense from her manner that she had read the mail. Ravi knew everything and thus went out of the library after greeting her. I look at her and quite uncomfortably said.

"Hi Pia."

"I read your mail," she replied in a jiffy.

"Why did you mail me like that," she continued and I did not know what had happened to me.

I looked at her and then bowed my head. I had no answer for her question. Quite hesitatingly I mustered the courage and said,

"What happened Pia? Did I write anything wrong?" I said and looked at her.

"I had been trying to tell you this for a long time Pia but never had the courage. It has taken me years to express my feelings but it is true. I am in love with you since the time we had met.

Whatever I have written is true Pia." I said in one breadth.

"But Rahul, I have always considered you as my best friend. I like your company. I have enjoyed every moment with you but I have never thought of you like that." She said and I felt a kind of sensation around my feet.

It was as if, the earth was revolving around me. I looked at her and then looked beneath. It was as if my mouth had been sealed. I did not know what to do when she said,

"I am really sorry, Rahul. I do not know if I could do that." She said and kept mum for a minute.

"I am sorry Pia. I never intended to hurt you. If this act of mine has hurt you, I apologize. I said as I saw her quite embarrassed with my act and went out of the library.

WHEN SHE FINALLY SAY..........I LOVE YOU

Since the time I had proposed her, my love story, kept swinging like a pendulum. Sometimes it comes near me and the next moment goes farthest from me. I, like a moron, kept looking at it moving from one end to another. It had been over two weeks since we had that conversation in the library. We had met a few times after that episode but the same comfort level had gone. We had not been as comfortable facing each other as before. I had been trying to avoid meeting her and would silently slipped away from the class as soon as it gets over.

Most of the times, I wanted not to come face to face with her and had tried to curtailed my encounter with her. I was wrong; we just could not remain good friends after what had happened two weeks before. It was not really the same as before. We had not been talking over phone. I had been trying to curtail going out in-group as I would have to face her and that would be quite an embarrassing for both of us. That one mail of mine had actually affected all of us. I had been trying to avoid her as much as possible. I would go to institute only to attend my preparation for GD as result for written test had started to come. I had messed up in love and thus I did not want to repeat the same in life. For the first time I had a purpose in life. I had learnt it from her only. How in place of how happy and contend my parents were seeing me working hard to attain something. They had never been so happy. For the first time, they believe that I could achieve something. I did not want to disappoint them again and thus wanted to forget what had happened between Pia and I. I want start afresh and put all my energy till the time I cleared final frontiers. Thank god, I had expressed everything that day. It would have been a disaster had I kept that in my heart, as I would not have been able to concentrate for my interview. Everything happens at the right time I believe. I had been trying hard to convince myself not to think about the past and concentrate on the next challenge that I had been going to face. One fine evening, while sitting at home, I got a call,

"Hi Rahul," I know this voice the moment I received the receiver.

"Hey Pia, how are you." I murmured the moment I heard that.

"I am fine. How are you." She replied and kept silent.

"Gr8!! So how it all going." I had nothing else to ask.

Fine, how was your SIBM interview? She asked as I had returned after attending my SIBM interview a day before.

"It was good. I could not do well in the psychological test though but recovered well in GD and interview." I replied and kept silent.

And….And, we both spoke together.

Ok, you tell me, when are you going to Pune." I asked as she had to leave for Pune for one of her exams.

We had not been talking so regularly but I used to get all the information as in what she had been upto, thanks to my good friends. They had been updating me with all the happenings.

"Tomorrow. I am leaving tomorrow morning." She replied and after a few second and a long breadth said.

"I am sorry."

"What, why do you feel sorry Pia." I said quite surprisingly.

"It could have been better. I should not have reacted that way." She said and kept silent again.

"I should have been more considerate. Since that time, I have been feeling a kind of vacuum in my life ." She continued and I felt a kind of great relief.

"She had not forgotten me. My mail had a late reaction." I thought.

"It's ok Pia. Even I should say sorry. I should not have sent that mail. But….i stopped in between.

But what Rahul." She asked immediately.

"I mean, I had no other option but to tell you Pia. I had been struggling for a long time to say this. We were good friends. We used to like each other's company. We couldn't slept until we talked atleast once in a day. I had been addicted to your presence." I continued for a minute since I did not want to waste this opportunity.

"I felt as if you also like me and I could not stop myself from doing that." I stopped.

"You know Rahul." She said abruptly.

"You know Rahul, I don't know what had happened to me when I read your mail. I was not expecting it may be." She said and I could feel her breadth beating faster than normal.

"Since the time, you have been away from me, I had not been felt good. Its always feel like something is missing in my life. I did try to forget you but could not able to do so." She said abruptly and I remember every word that Namit had told while we were returning to our hotel.

"Bloody, he is really a genius in the matter related to love." I paused for a second and felt on top of the world.

She had indirectly accepted me, I thought.

"So now what Pia." I tried to poke her further.

"I will tell you once I return from Pune. But one thing is sure, I now understand Newton's third law of motion." She said and I knew from whatever knowledge of Physics I had that my action has resulted with a positive reaction from her. God, I had been dying to hear this. Before, I could ask her further, she disconnected the phone.

God, I just don't know why girls do that. They would always keep us guessing.

Man what a relief that was. I could not believe my ears. I knew, my mail had done the trick. I could not hold my happiness and went to dialed Asad number. I did not want to waste a single second for my happiness to come out. It had been inside me for a long time.

Hey man. I am so happy today." I exclaimed the moment he picked up the phone.

"Why, did she call you?"

"God, he had same thing in mind as I." I paused.

"Yup, and….", I stopped and took a long breadth.

"And what…?"

"And she loves me."

"Heyyyy….congratulation." bloody he was more happier than me.

"Thanks, what a relief man. I feel like I am at top of the world."

"Yup, enjoy the moment buddy. You have suffered a lot lately. Just hold it to you."

I had the best ever sleep in last fifteen days. I would not forget that evening. Next morning, I had the same feeling for going to the institute which I had been trying to avoid after what had happened. Everything seemed perfect. I got up early. Had my breakfast and went to the institute. Before I reached there, my love story had already been published. I had the best day of my life and I was waiting desperately for her to come back. Fifteen days had passed without talking to her but after her call, it was very difficult to pass even a second without her. I had become restless. I wanted that days and night passed rapidly and she come back soon. Three days had passed since we had talk last. Two more days and she would be here. That evening Ravi and I had gone to check our mail when I saw her mail in my inbox,

Dear Rahul,

I have been away from you for three days but it feels like for ages we have not met. I want to come back to you as early as possible. I would not be able to write much as uncle is standing outside and waiting for me to come. I had just come to write you that how much I am missing you here. I love you Rahul and I want to see you soon. Please wait for me.

Yours ever

Pia

I kept looking at the screen when Ravi came near to me. He also read the mail. He looked at me and we kept on looking at the silver screen. She had replied my mail at the same manner as I had. It was a great feeling. I wanted to thank the person who invented internet. Bloody, he would never think that this discovery of him would come so handy in matters of love also.

Anyway, I was in cloud nine and was eagerly waiting for her to return.

BANANA BAR!!!

"Why the fuck did you came out of the bar?" Priyesh exclaimed.

"Bloody, I have never been to a place like that before." Ravi responded.

"Do you think we are the regulars'?" he shouted back.

"Didn't you like those scantily dressed women? They looked so sexy!" He retorted.

"Men, we have come here for a purpose but I believe you have no interest in that. You are wasting your time on all these craps." Ravi shouted.

"Can't we go to some other place." He continued.

I stood silent during the entire conversation, as I knew speaking here could start world war III.

We were in Mumbai for one of our exams. We had been to

Mumbai for the first time. We had heard a lot about it. Other then the home to bollywood, it offers a magnificent night lives. We have heard a lot about the dance bars, pubs and pulsating discotheque. Mere mention of Mumbai was enough for us to go into the dreams of a place where we could find all the stars we see and idolize in our life. What would happen if we come across one of the bollywood star?

In fact, going to Mumbai was not an unanimous choice. There was a lot of discussion on the matter. Ruchika had already booked her ticket for Nagpur. She had asked us though regarding this but most of us was reluctant to go to Mumbai. Asad wanted to come with us but his heart was not ready to move without Ruchika. It was always a one sided love for his. We all knew that Ruchika just consider him as a good friend and she does not have any interest in any other relationship with him. But, poor Asad, he keeps on following her wherever she goes in anticipation that one day she would accept him. We as a good Samaritan, allowed him to accompany her to Nagpur and as usual Namit joined them. Priyesh, Ravi and I boarded the train to Mumbai. I would not say that Pia was coming along with us as she was traveling with her dad and also was in an AC compartment. We had though decided to meet in Mumbai as that was the first journey we were taking after our decision to become a couple.

It was the month of April, when most part of the country had started to grapple with the heat.

Journey to Mumbai was twenty-eight hours from the place we

had started. Sitting on the Non-AC compartment was not helping our cause either. But, that is the price we had to pay for belonging to an average middle class families. Priyesh had to pay the price of being a friend of us as he had to travel on Non-AC even though he could easily afford an AC ticket.

"Fucking, this train runs so slow. Moreover, it stops at every station." Priyesh exclaimed in anger.

"Welcome to Indian railway. Hope you would reach your destination safely in next twenty-eight hours, if train runs on time." Ravi joked.

Can you believe it still takes twenty-eight hours to reach a destination of 1800 Kms. That is approximately 65 Kms per hour. Fucking, trains across the globe runs almost double in speed on an average, in compare to us. His mathematics brain calculated.

But, boss look at the size of our country and the numbers of trains that runs everyday. They have to set the timing as per the situation and availability. I said as if to calm things down.

Moreover, the infrastructure is not at per to support such a speed in the country." I continued.

This intellectual conversation continued for some time and more people joined in the conversation. This is always the case while you move in a train. Any talk would take center stage and more and more people join to display his intelligence on the matter. Sometimes, it becomes like we are participating in a group discussion and a big prize is waiting to grab. But it is quite interesting as this helps in pass the time and for that matter, to know many insights on the subject of discussion. It was hot inside the compartment and all these socalled fans were of no use. I sometime wonder why the hell they put fans as most of the time they run as if someone trying to squeeze the lemon so hard to get even the last drop of juice. To add to the misery, they sometimes never run at all. Moreover, I always found, the three fans are not at all sufficient for the people of eight in an enclosure. The direction of the fans is not at all serving any purpose but who cares; at least they have done their job. After all, none of the VIP really boards a non-ac compartment, and all of us, the middle class people do not really deserve to be in the comfort zone. We are born to live in misery and discomfort. After all, we are not the one who is shaping the country. Do not know how many bottles of cold water we were gulping down the throat. That was the only source of cooling effects that we could afford there.

The conversation varied from politics to sports to our day-to-day struggle for survival. It was dawn of the evening and light breeze was coming from the windows which was making life a bit comfortable. Although I was there, some part of me was still thinking about someone sitting just 3 compartments away from us. What would she be thinking? Would she missing me? It would have been so nice if she were coming with us. I was thinking about the time when we were returning from the picnic. She had been sitting so close to me. Today, while gong to the same destination, I could not even see her. I was looking outside the window in the thoughts when priyesh hopped and sit beside me.

So buddy, thinking about her." he said in excitement.

Oh no. not at all, I was just looking outside and wondering about the abundance of beauties that lies in our country." I tried to shift the conversation from her.

Ohoho...you cannot hide your emotion even if you try my boy." He said quite mischievously.

Bloody, sometime he behaves so irritatingly." I paused.

Cmon lets go to her compartment." He continues and I could not believe him.

You are gonna mad. You know she is traveling with her dad." I replied quite irritatingly.

He is right Priyesh. It would not be wise to go there specially because she is with her father."

Ravi interfered.

Don't worry, I will talk to her father. You people just sit with me there." He remain persistent.

"At least we could be away from this fucking heat for some time.

Also, could you see how much my lover boy missing his lady love" He continued and we just do not paid any heed to his words.

Think, what she must be doing without him. At least we could provide our beautiful couple some time to relish this journey." He tried to reason with Ravi.

"No way, I am not going. You people go. Moreover, I am comfortable here."

"Bloody, you do not care for your friend. I have come with you in this fucking train and you are not doing me this small favor", He tried to blackmail us.

Actually, he was right. I was desperately missing someone. I wanted to go near her and enjoy what I called the first journey of us together. I wanted to hold her and enjoy this beautiful countryside of this beautiful country. On more cajoling from him, I could not stop myself and agreed to go to her compartment.

In next few seconds, we were heading towards her compartment. I was a bit anxious though as in how am going to face her dad especially in front of her. What would she thinks while seeing us there? Would she be angry by seeing us there? I knew she would not like to let her father know about our relationship at this juncture. Moreover, it's been not long that we have been dating. I just could not think of my life without her. I do not want to lend her in any kind of trouble.

"Bloody, look at the environment. It's so cool and calm and we are sitting in an oven." Priyesh exclaimed the moment we entered into her AC compartment.

"So you should have booked an AC compartment na. Why the fuck did you come with us poor people." I replied.

It was almost 7'o clock in the evening when we reached her seat number. She was reading a magazine and was almost surprised to see us there.

"Hey, you all are here." She somehow managed to ask and I could not stop myself glancing at her.

"Yeah, we were getting bored sitting there and thus decided to stroll down the train." Priyesh immediately reply and I saw her getting up folding the magazine closed.

"Dad, they are my batch mates". She introduced us to her dad. We sat on whatever vacant space we saw nearby.

For a few seconds we remained silent when her father asked us.

"So you all are going to Mumbai?"

"Yes, and this train also going to Mumbai." I thought but could not say the same.

"Yes uncle, we also going to appe ar for the same exam. Ravi intervene before I could spoke anything."

That's so nice.

Her dad turned out to be a very nice man. That was the first time we had met. But, he behaved as if we are quite familiar. He offered us tea and asked where we would stay in Mumbai. I think, that was the first good question anyone asked us during the entire journey.

"Actually, I have a cousin there, who lives in Borivali. We would first go there and see if we can stay for some time." Ravi answer.

"Bloody, he never told us about his cousin." I thought

But he is Ravi. We always expect such mystery from his arms.

After all, he is not the one, who does not make plan. We knew he had all the plans as in where we are going to stay. We had no options but to nod our head in agreement.

"That is all right." It is always good to have someone in a city like

Mumbai. Even we would stay at one of my cousin who has been living in Mumbai for long." He replied.

"I wished I could stay with them. At least I would spend some more time with her." I ponder.

"But in case, you need accommodation, look near VT station as there are many good and cheap hotels around." He continued.

"Bloody, cant you say, come along with us." I thought with a grim smile.

I looked at Pia. She was smiling. Perhaps she was smiling at my ignorance in front of her dad. I was the one who kept silent most of the time and was looking quite uncomfortable there. She had perhaps sensed my anxiety. I could see her making faces through her eyes and mouth behind her dad while they were engaged in conversation. I on the other hand am trying to avoid the eye contact and most of the time looking below. Priyesh and Ravi kept on talking to her dad and that helped us to share some good moments in silence. She looked so nice while doing such act. By the time, many in the areas started to feel uneasy, as we had occupied most of their seat. We decided to take a leave and stood to move towards our oven as per Priyesh.

She stood and took her dad's permission to see us off. While crossing the compartment, she holds my hand tightly, pulled me aside almost towards the door and planted a gentle kiss on my lips.

"Thank you shona, I was just missing you." She said and quickly returned towards her seat.

Before I could react, she was gone. I could not believe what had happened. I kept on standing like that for some time. I had not thought that something like that would happened and that too in a running train. We had our first kiss. I silently came towards my seat and sat as if nothing has happened.

"So, how was it?" Priyesh jumped over me almost pushing me to the back of seat.

"What?" I replied in anticipation that he might be asking about the kiss.

"I mean, how was the meeting?" he smiled and I took a sigh of relief perhaps knowing that they did not see what had just happened.

"Yeah, great!!! Thanks." I replied and kept silent.

"So now the diner is from your side." He continues.

Yeah sure!!!" I could have given him whatever they had asked at that point of time.

The feeling had not sink in yet. I was in a state of shock and was not reacting in the same manner as before. I just wanted to relish the moment in silent.

Soon we had our diner. By that time most of the people had started to go into slumber. It would have been unwise to continue our conversation as that would have made many people uncomfortable. Thus we also decided to go for sleep.

"So, you didn't say how was the kiss." Priyesh smiled at me while going up to his birth.

"Shut up!!! Go to hell." I could only reply when I see a cute smile on Ravi, s face.

Bloody, they had seen it.

Anyway, I had the time of my life and I wanted to relish it. I keep on thinking about the incident for long only to wake up by the noise of morning tea stalls vendor. It was dawn of a new day.

"You nut; you never told us that we are going to stay in your cousin's place." Priyesh yelled at Ravi while sipping the morning tea We had almost forgotten it last night.

"But, you never asked me." He smiled.

"So now, we could save some more money for our enjoyment."

His calculation started again.

Really, if you were in the company of a businessperson, you would end up doing pluses and minuses.

"Yes, so do not forget to treat me." Ravi said.

"Do not worry jaan, we would give you a treat, you would never forget." Priyesh replied in his mischievous style and I could sense he would do something which would irks him.

I know him. There must be something crappy going through his mind. After all, he just cannot be so good to Ravi. He would surely do something that irks him.

"We should reach Mumbai in next 10 hours. Have you talked to your cousin as in where we had to get down." I quizzed Ravi.

"Yes sir, we should reach Mumbai by 9 pm. We had to get down at Dadar station. Borivali is on the western line. We would catch the borivali fast local from Dadar and would reach borivali by 10.30 if everything runs on time." He answers in one shot. He had done the full homework.

"Impressive, well done Mate." I appreciated.

"My cousin would wait for us at the borivali station." He said.

"But, have you told him that we are three. I have heard, it is very difficult to have a proper home in Mumbai, especially for a salaried people." I enquired.

"Don't worry, I have told him I have never visited them but I hope that would be sufficient for us. They are two, which makes five of us. Moreover, it is just the matter of 4 days. In worst case, if it were not comfortable, we would shift to some hotel. Not a big deal." He responded.

I believed, he was right as anyway we would reach Mumbai at night and would probably not get any accommodation.

We reached Mumbai one and a half hours late. That means, at 10.30 pm. That was good enough keeping in mind the history of Indian railway when it comes to timings. Anyway, we got down at the Dadar station and had the first encounter with the city of dreams. Pia did not get down at the Dadar station as they had to go to VT. We had decided to meet day after tomorrow after our exam. It was thirty minutes past ten and station was filled with people. I could see almost everyone running to catch the train. We had never experience such a mad rush at the railway station. There were long queue at the ticket counter. At last we got our ticket and move to board the borivali fast. We asked the vendor for the right platform and moved there. We had heard of separate first class compartment and thus decided to ask where to stand for second class compartment. Platform was full of people grappling with one another to stay ahead to board the train.

"How the fuck we board the train?" Priyesh shouted.

"You need not board the train. Just be in the line. You would board automatically." I narrated what I had heard of.

"Can't we go by some other mode?" he quizzed.

"Yes we could, but that would be fucking costly and would take more time." Ravi interferes.

"This is the easiest and the cheapest mode of traveling." He continued.

"If this is the easiest, what would we expect to the hardest." Priyesh exclaimed.

Soon, we saw train arriving at the platform. People started to push one another before train take a halt. It was like a commotion. I have never seen such frenzy at any of our station.

"Get ready guys, we have to board this train. We have just a few seconds." I exclaimed.

"But how could we board. We have our bags also." Priyesh shouted

"Just be in line and put all your energy." I responded.

"Where the hell is the energy man! I have lost all that in that fucking train." He shouted.

By that time, train arrived at the platform and we had no option but to board it in whatever ways we could. Somehow, we managed to rushed in. we could hardly seen one another. So I asked if everyone boarded or not. They said yes. Now started the toughest journey of our life.

We could hardly stand on the train. Moreover, there were no place to keep our bags. Bloody, how could I hold this bag. It is so painful Where the hell you put me." Priyesh shouted angrily.

"You want to get down at Parel." One asked.

"No, we have to go to Borivali." I responded.

"Then why are you are standing at the gate? Go in side?" He chided

"But how could we go inside. It was too crowded to even take a good breadth. At every station, we were struggled to cope with this question. Bloody, a few people is getting down while more rushing in." where the hell they are coming from." I thought in disgust.

The compartment was stinking like a hell. Moreover, the fans are not working. Why the hell they put fans? I thought again

Anyway, in an hour or so we somehow managed to reached borivali. It was again a mad rush to get down. Finally, we landed safely. It was a great sigh of relief.

"Man, I would never travel with you guys. I was almost dead" Priyesh shouted He was right. I have never traveled in such a crowded train before. How could they face it everyday? I pondered.

Soon, we met with Ravi's cousin. He introduced us to him.

"How was the journey?" He asked.

"Do not ask brother. It was hell of a journey." Priyesh just could not stop himself.

"Yeah I can understand. We do it every day." He paused.

"We must have taken the first class ticket. At least that would be better." Ravi said after a long time.

"It is no different brother. Only difference that I could feel while traveling in a first class compartment is that, you got the smell of a perfume instead of perspiration." He tried to clear things.

"Anyway, you people must be hungry. Let's take some food from here as most of the restaurants would have closed by now." He said and went towards a small hotel.

Finally, we reached his place. It was a small one room apartment Probably in a 600 square feet area. It was sufficient for two but not at all sufficient for five people.

"Welcome to my den guys. I know it is not big enough but it is very precious for us." He said quite honestly.

"This is my friend Kamal and two of us lives in this palace." He said as we shook hand with Kamal.

"It is really beautiful. At least you have a home to live in this big city." I replied.

"Moreover, it is so nice of you two to welcome us and that is what matters." I continued.

Priyesh was not happy as it appears from his face but he had no option but to nod in agreement. In fact, we had no option to go somewhere else at this point of time. We were so drained out of energy and just wanted to take a sleep.

"I am sorry guys. We all have to sleep on floor." Kamal said hiding his emotion.

"No problem sir. Let us make arrangement as we are just dying to sleep." As soon as we lied on bed, we got up only in the morning and at around 10 am. That spoke volumes of how tired we were.

That was the first morning in the city we had heard a lot. Soon, we were offered a cup of coffee.

It was so nice of them. They were doing everything to make us comfortable but we knew it would be tough to stay there for long. Moreover, we had no idea how far the examination center was. Therefore, we decided to go and check it. We could also see some of the city by doing so. As soon as we left, Priyesh said quite gentlemanly as if we would be comfortable there. In fact, he wanted us to shift somewhere else.

"Man, I believe we should move to a hotel" He said.

"It would be tough on them. Moreover, how could we travel for our exam", he continued".

Actually, he was right which we soon found out when we reach our examination center. It was far away from the place. Travelling from Borivali to Chembur, moreover on peak hour would be a tough challenge for us. Therefore, we decided to shift to a place nearby.

On our examination day, we reached to the examination center way before the schedule time.

That is always the case with us. We had appeared in so many examinations and on all occasion reached our center almost two hours before the schedule start of exam. This is not because of any real motive but in all the cases we were quite scared of reaching the venue late. We had this fear psychosis that we would end up meeting some unexpected events and would reach our examination late. This has not happened so far but as usual we were in the examination center almost two hours before the schedule start. This time it was really painful. We had our examination center in a government senior secondary school in Chembur. The sun was almost over our heads and we had nowhere to go. There was almost non existence of any place where we could go and spend some time before the exam. Fortunately, there was a tea vendor at some distance and we spent almost one and half hour sipping innumerable tea and for breakfast took bread butter at the stall. On reaching the venue half an hour before the start I found Pia at one corner in conversation with a middle aged man. She had just arrived for the exam and I could see her happiness seeing me coming towards her along with Ravi and Priyesh.

"Hey, you people have just reached?" She immediately asked the moment we reached near her.

"No, as usual we had come way before time and thus were enjoying hot cups of tea in this heat and humidity." Priyesh explained before us and I could see her dimple smile.

"Oh, but why do you people always reach before time".

"Anyway, this is my cousin Rupesh. He had come with me to the examination center." She introduced her cousin to us.

"Bloody, her dad would not let her do anything alone", I grinned.

"So you would go back with him only" Priyesh asked instantly.

"We had thought if we could go somewhere after the exam", he continued.

"No probs, we would go after the exam only when you people take me home by 8 in the evening." She replied and looked at me in amazement.

"No probs mam!!! We will be at your service" Priyesh would never leave his banter.

"Boss, we should go inside the hall now. It is open and people are entering." Ravi intervenes and we all proceed towards the hall and to our respective rooms for the examination.

Next two hours passed in a jiffy. I sometime wonder if the speed of time increases while giving an examination. I always found it to be over in a jiffy. Anyway, we came out of the examination center. In comparison to other examinations that I had taken, I believe, I had done better and I found no reason to be disappointed with the effort. But, as usual, I moan in the prospects of making a few more attempts had I have more time. I could see a little disappointment in

Pia's face and I could sense that she had not done well.

"Hey, how was the exam?" I asked her the moment she came rushing towards me.

"Not bad, but I believe I could have done better." She replied.

"Do not worry. It is human. We always thinks that we could have done better. I know you have done well." I tried to sooth her nerves

"What about you Ravi?" she asked him.

"Well, I think I have done better than other examinations." He said and I have no doubt that he had done better then all of us.

It is pointless to ask Priyesh as he would never give us the right answer. He would just say,

"Cmon yaar, forget it. It was just an exam."

It was almost 1 pm when we decided to go for lunch and move for some sightseeing afterwards. Her cousin had left before the exam and we had to take her back home before 8 in the evening. I was eagerly waiting for this moment. After all, we would be together at a place where none know us and we could easily roam around the city without any apprehension of being caught by our family and friends which always the case in a small city.

"So, where are you taking me dear?", she asked me holding my hand.

"Not you only, where are you taking us man?", Priyesh would always wait for such moments.

"I do not know about you people, but we are going towards Marine drive." I responded.

"I have heard a lot about the place and even seen it on television. It just looks awesome."

I was in a state of dilemma. I could not asked Ravi to be with Priyesh till the time I am with her knowing his chemistry with Priyesh. They were poles apart and it would be almost difficult to keep them together for long.

"C'mon Priyesh, let them go to Marine Drive. We would go somewhere else." I was absolutely amazed to hear this from Ravi.

Perhaps he had understood my dilemma. It was so nice of him to take this horrific decision as I knew Priyesh would not remain good with him. He would certainly do things which could not go down his sleeves.

On second thought I let them go with a promise as we would meet near Gateway of India by 7.30 in the evening. I did not want to waste this opportunity to be with Pia, especially spending time with her on the bank of Arabian sea. It would be so romantic to walk along the marine drive by holding her hands and eating all those roadside stuffs. It would be all so like movie.

"Why did you send them away?" Pia asked me as soon as we reached there.

They had dropped us near marine drive and had gone towards Gateway.

"I wanted to be with you dear. Just you and me, under the sun, walking along the sea, our first date together in a city which gives hopes to millions of couples around the world through magnificent movies from bollywood", I was explaining to her like a true bollywood hero.

"Oh, that's so romantic. I never knew that you are such a romantic person." She winked at me.

"What else have you learnt from bollywood movies." She smiled at me and I could not do anything else except return her with the smile.

I kept silent for a while and bought her a bunch of roses.

By that time, the sun had started to disappear from the sky. Evening was fast engulfing. The sunset at the marine drive is an experience in itself. By then, a number of couples had occupied most of the place and sat silently on the upper part of pavement and enjoying the sight of the sunset holding their beloved one in the arms. We could not resist the temptation and sat on some vacant space on the pavement looking at the sunset. She kept her head on my shoulders and I wrapped my arms around her and hold her tightly. The arrival of a little shades of darkness coupled with some light breeze had made the environment absolutely amazing. With every passing second, I could hear the palpation. It was beating faster. She had almost clutched me around my neck. I could hear her breadth and in a moment we were enjoying the silence of the time. We kissed and kissed again ignoring the sound of water and passerby. We were the two birds in love away from the world enjoying the moment. The frequent shreds of water particles sprinkles after colliding with wall did not deter us either and for a few moments we were absolutely out of the world.

By the time we realized, it was already 7.30 in the evening. We had planned to meet Priyesh and Ravi at the gateway. They must be waiting at the Gateway. In a hurry, we caught a cab nearby and moved towards the Gateway for what, I believe, the end of the most memorable evening of our life.

THE NIGHT SOMETHING DIED!!!

I had called at Priyesh's home many times in last one week and had not received a satisfactory answer as in where he had been for a month. On many occasion, I did not find any answer at all. On one occasion I did go at his place and found the door closed from outside. I asked his neighborhood and found that they had been gone to his ancestral place a day before. Many attempts of mine to find his whereabouts have failed. I did get to know that he has been in Purulia and would return soon. Of course, nothing had gone right on our farewell night, but things could have been sorted out. Final results were announced and our fate was sealed. Some had got the desire institutes while many had to contend with whatever they had got. Ravi had moved to Mumbai just day after the farewell and Ruchika is about to leave for Jaipur. She had not contacted anyone after what had happened the farewell night. We had tried to meet her though but in all effort, she refused to meet any one of us. Namit and Asad were leaving for Pune next week and fortunately Pia and I had got admission in Kolkata, though in different institutes. Rishi was the last one to move to Pune. Priyesh had failed to qualify in any of the institute and thus we had restrained ourselves to a minimum celebration as almost all of us were expecting something for him. I had observed a peculiar behavior in Priyesh for some time before the declaration of results. He had proposed to Ruchika a week before and as expected had been declined quite politely by her. I knew he is the kind of person who would not be affected with it in any way keeping in mind his track record with girls. I thought it would be a little embarrassing for him as he thought she like him and thus he would be fine within a few days. I also knew that his not making into any of the institute had little effect on him. Only concern that I had was he would a little disturbed with the fact that we would not be with him in a few days. He would be alone in the city in which he had enjoyed most of his times with us.

Perhaps that feeling of loneliness had been troubling him. We had been invited by our coaching institute for a get together at the roof top of the building.

It has been a ritual since the times, the institute came into being. Every year they throw a big farewell party to the students who had qualified as well as who had not.

We were keen to join the party but not without Priyesh. He agreed to come along with us only when we blackmailed him that we will not go until he accompanied us to the farewell party.

"Hi man!!! Checking out the girls?", I poked him on seeing him watching the proceedings from a distance.

"You could propose Ruchika one more time before she leaves from here." I tried to perk him a bit and took another glass of cold drink.

There are few people who had been drinking beer. Most of us had never touch alcohol and thus was very happy to enjoy the evening with cold drinks.

I knew he would not dare to propose her again.

He smiled a bit and took a long sip of beer.

"C'mon man, cheer up. What is the problem? You never seemed so out of a place like this" I tried to cheer him up.

"Tell me, you are ok?", I asked on a serious note.

"Yeah man!! Just not feeling well." He finally spoke.

I had never seen him so depressed ever. It has been over a year that I had known him, and every time he seems to be in a mood of enjoyment. He always uses to find happiness in little things. The usual sense of enjoyment has gone. I was expecting some witty remarks from him. A number of times I had to interfere to save him from putting himself in the midst of trouble.

Since the time result has come out, he has not been in the best frame of mind. He was happy for us but somewhere he had been hurt by his failure. I did not try to force him further and move towards Namit and Asad.

"Hey man, so finally it's time to say good bye." I poked them once I reach there.

"Yeah, it's time to move apart. I feel so nostalgic." Namit reacted.

"Hahaha, we have still not moved and you are feeling nostalgic. How would you survive there." I said moving my hand on his shoulders.

"Yeah man, it's just a week and we will be heading towards different direction. I feel so sad thinking that we would not be able to meet so often now", he lamented.

"Look at the positive side man. Imagine, we would come after many months and meet like this.

It would be great fun." Asad jumped into the conversation

From a distance, I saw Priyesh was having a conversation with Ruchika.

Hey Asad, look there, it is time you go and tell her your feelings or she would go with Priyesh." I tried to take a dig with Asad.

"Haan haan beta, go hurry up before she flies with him." Namit joined in the fun.

"C'mon, we are just good friends." He smiled and turns his eyes away from them.

We were having a nice conversation when sudden sound of broken glass pulled our senses towards the direction where Ruchika and Priyesh were having a conversation.

"I mean it Ruchika, I love you very much." We could see Priyesh begging her and holding her tightly with both his hands.

"You are drunk. Leave me priyesh. We will talk tomorrow." She was trying to remove herself from his clutches.

"We are good friends. I never had any such feelings for you, Priyesh. I have told you several times this. Why don't you understand?" She screamed and we rushed towards them.

Everyone had by then turned towards them and I could see the embarrassment on Ruchika's face.

"But I love you. I cannot live without you Ruchika. Look at me. I have not been living my life by merely thinking that I would not be able to be with you. Please don't do this to me." the alcohol contents had taken over him.

I could see blood coming out of his hand. Perhaps he had been injured by the broken glass.

"You have gone mad. I am going", and she turned towards the exit wiping her tears.

He immediately stood on his feet and jumped towards her.

"No, you cannot go without answering me." he screamed holding her shoulders from both his hands and I could easily see the anger on his eyes of having faced rejection.

"Leave her Priyesh." Before we moved towards them, Asad jumped on to him and pushed him to a corner. He fell on the table nearby thus toppled whatever drinks remain over the table.

113

We rushed towards them before it would go out of control.

You bloddy, how dare you push me like that." He shouted and ran towards Asad What the hell you people doing here.? I held Priyesh over there and shouted to save them from any further embarrassment. Almost everyone was on shocked to see such a behavior from him.

I never thought that he would ever conduct himself in such manner leave apart creating a drama amongst all of us.

Leave me Rahul, I will kill him. He has pushed me." he was getting furious with every passing second. The alcohol had taken his senses away for the moment.

I know what has been going on between them. You fucker, you had been sleeping around with her." he had crossed all the limits.

Ruchika just could not stand and ran towards the exit. I saw Pia and Ravi followed her.

Before, I could say something, Asad came rushing and planted a tight slap on his face. He had been stopped by a few people who had been mere spectators during the entire episode.

I saw priyesh vomiting profusely. He had been drunk a lot I believe. Asad and Namit had already left from the place and I was the only one who could take him to the doctor in case he required medicine. None would offered him any sympathy after what they had been witnessed. I had no option but to be with him. I saw people leaving the venue in a jiffy. It had been the worst end to a very beautiful night. Within a fortnight, we all headed towards our respective destination though not as we would have liked to.

NEW CITIES, NEW BEGINNING!!!

It has been almost over one month since we had moved to our respective destination. In last one month, other than a few mails from Ravi, I had not heard anything from anyone else. It could be probably because; they had all been trying to settle at their respective places. I could understand as I myself had little time to enjoy after the hectic classes are over. Moreover, being the new entrants we had little access to the systems and procedure and in some cases we used to have almost no access of internet for weeks. In fact, we could not muster the courage to go near the computer lab on account of fear for ragging. The moment class gets over; we used to run towards the hostel into the confines of our rooms to avoid the eye contact with seniors. I almost for a week could not meet Pia even though she was in the same city and in close vicinity from my place. After only a week, I found time to go to her and we met. I had gone to her hostel one evening and we met over a cup of coffee to her hostel mess.

Next few weeks passed over like this. We had got over our foundation and a big celebration happened where seniors threw a welcome party for all the juniors. The ragging session over and it is the time the difference between seniors and juniors over for better. We had become friends. I had invited Pia onto our welcome party.

Hey, are you comfortable here." I asked her seeing her not in a mood of enjoyment.

Yup! Am alright!! She replied.

Cmon, I introduced you to my friends." I said and took her to some of my friends with whom I had whatever friendship in these couple of months.

She met with Shreya, abhinav and Tulika.

You seemed to be very favorites with girls." She asked me and gave a shy smile Hahaha!! Why did you asked this." I asked looking at her.

You didn't like it.

Nope, I just asked casually. I believe they seemed to be quite happy meeting you.

I have spoiled your day. They would not come near you if they come to know you have a girl friend." She winked at me.

I would be very happy if this happens. I can not think anyone beyond you." I replied quite seriously.

You become so serious. Cmon, I was just joking." She hold my hand and I kept my hand across her shoulders.

Party was gradually getting hotter and most of the people were started to dance the night out.

I was enjoying the quite moment with Pia as we had met after a long time since we had moved to Kolkata.

Did you get to speak to any one else? She asked.

"Yeah, I received a few mails from Ravi and Asad but not from Ruchika", I said and moved to get one more glass of coke.

"Yeah, since that night she has gone into hibernation. She has not even contacted me." she said".

"Perhaps we could ask her as in how she has been?" She continued.

"Don't worry, honey she would be alright. I would write to her tomorrow", I said and glanced at her.

"Hey Rahul, come on to dance floor." Shreya was calling from a distance.

We went onto the dance floor and for the first time, I had the company of the women I always wanted to, moreover on the dance floor.

The night continued for a longer period but we had to move as Pia had to return to her hostel before the schedule time and I did not want her to be late.

Next evening after the class, I went to the computer lab and wrote mails to each one of my friends with whom we had shared the most precious moment of my life. I knew they all would have been enjoying this moment for which they all had worked very hard. I wrote to Ruchika about how she had been and what has been going on in her life. She had replied the next day and I could sense she had not been gotten over of what had happened that night. She gave me her number though and I had replied to call her as soon as possible.

Next Saturday, Pia and I had gone to watch a movie. I told her about Ruchika and we decided to call her on the given number.

Pia dialed her hostel number and it was busy. We dialed a few times more when someone picked up the phone.

"Hello, can I speak to Ruchika." I asked the lady who received the phone.

Which Ruchika. Ruchika Sharma or Ruchika Dayal." She mumbled over the phone.

"R…uchika Sharma", I said hurriedly.

One moment please, she left the phone and went to call her.

I could hear some of the chirpy voices coming out of the phone. Perhaps it would have been the common room of their hostel. I let Pia hear some of the conversation and she snatched the receiver from me perhaps not to allowed me to hear all these girlie talks,

"Hey Ruchika. How are you madam?" She shouted in a few moments.

"Hey, I am fine. How are you doing? Long time" she replied.

"Ruchika, it's me. I had called you and not she." I tried to tease Pia.

"Hey you people. So nice to hear from you." She said.

"Yes, and you had forgotten all of us, right?" I replied.

"It's not like that Rahul. You know, I am just trying to cope with a new environment." She said in a soft voice.

"I can understand. By the way, how are things at your end." I replied casually.

"It's all good. Have adjusted to the environment and am really enjoying every moment of it." She seemed alright.

"Hey Ruchika, talk to me buddy. You just vanished from the scene. You didn't meet me while leaving Ranchi." Pia grabbed the receiver from me.

"Yeah honey, didn't feel like it. Nothing seemed right after that night." She replied melancholically.

"Yup, true. It was really bad. I hope you have forgotten everything." She tried to calm her.

They continued to talk for longer time as is the case with girls and I kept looking at the STD machine. The pulse rate seemed to be becoming faster.

That night, we strolled down the road at esplanade for a longer distance thinking about all that happened among us. One small act of Priyesh had created a great rift among all of us. The intensity with which we used to meet had gone in a jiffy. It had created among us a kind of gap which, it appeared, was not going to be filled in near future.

While returning after dropping Pia off to her hostel, I saw Shreya sitting alone at one corner of our hostel lawn. I went near her and sat beside her on the pavement.

"Hey, when did you come." She replied almost in a jiffy the moment she saw me.

"Just now, returning after dropping Pia to her hostel", I said.

Oh, that gr8!! You people are known to each other for long, right." She asked me.

Yup, almost 5 years. we have been together since then." I said quite proudly.

So, you have been in a relationship for five long years, exciting!!!" she said quite surprisingly.

Not exactly, we have done our graduation together, but its been just a year since we have been in a serious relationship." I clarified

Oh, thts really gr8!! She said.

We sat over there for a few minutes and went to our respective rooms thereafter. That was the start of the first of the many nights that we have spend over there discussing all about College, Home, Pia, us and many other things.

Time has been flying like anything and we had been enjoying every moment of it. Before we could realize it, the first semester examination had been announced. I for once thought that it would be going to be a cakewalk keeping in mind the kind of preparation that we had done to qualify for the entrance exam. It all seemed an uphill task the moment I saw the syllabus for the exam. Bloody it was a hell of a thing. However high I try I would not be able to complete the whole syllabus in time. For the first time I realize how important days I had lost in all these late night boozing and party session. I cursed my seniors who had told us to be relaxed and enjoy our stay in hostel. Bloody, who would come to our rescue now?

"Have you seen the syllabus for the exam?" I asked Shreya sitting on the same pavement one night

Yeah, its too much. I do not think I would be able to complete it." She replied.

Exactly, and I have heard they would not promote us to the next semester if we failed in maximum three subjects." I told her what I had heard.

"I am definitely going to be fail" she said.

"Hmmn, this is going to be one of the toughest days of our life, I believe.

"We need to get hold of some seniors and get all the notes that they had made" She said.

"They say, questions are repetitive and we just need to remember the answers and sit in the exam." She replied and it all seemed so easy.

"I hope so, otherwise I would not be able to cross this hurdle" I said casually and we moved towards the hostel.

I collected whatever notes I could get hold of and made sure to prepare every question that had come in previous semester exams. Shreya's was a great help and we made sure to discuss between us related topics before the exam. Pia also had her first semester exam and thus we had decided not to meet before the exams. The exam bug had entered into our hostel and all seemed to be preparing in full swing. The usual session at the common room had ended and we all had been concentrating hard for our exam. For once it all seemed like we had move backwards. We used to copy whatever notes we were able to gather. The room was filled with Xerox papers from almost everywhere. The first semester is always very important and I wanted to do well.

THAT ONE NIGHT.........

$2$1st July' 2002. I would not forget the night of 21st July. We had the declaration of our second semester examination. We had planned a big celebration at night to celebrate our promotion to the senior batch. We knew that as the senior batch is passing out, we would be the king of campus. We had a big celebration at the common room of our hostel. I was a new entrant to the club of drinkers and smokers and thus was waiting anxiously for the party to start. The celebration continues till the wee hours. Two pegs were enough for me to move away from the reality and enter the gate of heaven. I had drunk an extra peg though not because of the insistence of anybody as any social drinker claim but to prove a point that my capacity of alcohol consumption has increased. I had no idea what a large peg and a small peg meant at that point of time. Now when I understood the fact I believe I had consumed more than six large pegs that night. I did not know how

I went to my room and who accompanied me till the time I heard someone knocking at my door quite blatantly. I tried to ignore it many time as I thought it as a prank by fellow hostelites. As the sound increases, I had no option but to open it.

As soon as I opened the door, I saw our hostel security man standing tall with a bamboo in one hand and a towel draped around his neck. He had not changed his attire over the years.

"Kya hai?" I asked quite irritably.

"Sahib aapka phone hai pune se." he said hesitatingly.

I saw the time. It was 4 o' clock. Who had called me at this hour; I paused for a second and kept following the security man towards the reception of our hostel. At that time mobile phones were a luxury and selected few actually afford it. Most of us had to content with the landline phone installed at the reception of our hostel.

"Hello." I said in the dizziest way I could have.

"Rahul, Rishi has consumed the whole bottle of sleeping pills." Asad said quite hurriedly,

"What, when?" I jumped out of the chair like an agile man who had just regain his consciousness.

"What are you saying man. How is he?" I exclaimed trying to balance myself with the help of wall.

I was anticipating a better reply.

"I do not know, yaar. I got a call from his roommate. We have admitted him to city hospital." He tried to explain me.

126

"Doctor has flushed his stomach and stopped the poison to spread. He is still in ICU." He continue.

"Fuck man! Why did he do so?" I said in disbelief.

We are in hospital waiting for him to get consciousness. I hope everything is fine." Asad said calmly.

Do not worry yaar!! He will be alright." I tried to console and kept the phone with the promise that I will reach there soon.

I kept on sitting there for a while. I was totally lost.

Kya hua sahib." Security man asked as he saw me in pensive mood.

Kuch nahi." I said and went towards my room.

His face was revolving around my mind. I was lost in some thoughts. I recollected everything.

He is a dear friend of us. I have known him for almost two years. We had met at the coaching class during our preparation for IIM. In our first few interactions, we became good friends even though he was three years seniors to us. He never mentioned the tough times he had been undergone. Life had not been very kind to him. His was the perfect case of someone started well to reach to the top of mountain but lost in the middle in absence of correct guidance.

Being the only son of a middle class family did not help him either. He tried for medical entrance after securing good percentage in class XI but could not clear it. That was a big setback for a young boy who always dreamt of becoming a doctor and serves the poor and needy. At an age of 21, he started his own pharmacy store after doing his major in pharmacy. He wanted to have many such stores which run 24x7. Those days the concepts of such chain of pharmacy stores were unheard of. Perhaps his dream of serving the society was still alive. Despite having initial loses he continued with the idea of having branded pharmacy stores across the city.

Perhaps he could not understand the basic requirement of such branded stores as after running in loses for almost two years he was forced to shut down the business. By that time he had accrued heavy debt and thus went into depression. At that time his father somehow bailed him out of this debt by selling his ancestors property. He was in hibernation for almost a year. He had been saved from the verge of a major collapse.

With that heavy thought I went straight to the railway station to catch a train to Pune. I somehow managed a second class ticket and soon I was on my way to Pune. I had a major hangover as I could not be able to sleep the whole night after such a heavy drinking.

I lay myself on the upper birth of a second class compartment and throw myself to catch some much needed sleep. The occurrence of last night did not let me sleep and I kept on fighting for it. I was in total disbelief that anything like that had actually happened. What if it were a bad dream? I could not believe that a mature head like him could take such an extreme step. He had been very happy with the way things have started for him after the disaster. He thought that he has given a new life to make amend for the lost time. It has been over a years that he got admission in Pune University to pursue MBA. I had once visited the place since he got admission and found him absolutely happy. There is no sign of repentance for the past. I kept on thinking about him and do not know when I went into sleeping mode. A sudden brake has broken my slumber and I saw it was 8'o clock in the evening. I had got a good sleep. I saw the train halted at a station. I got down, stretch my body to the fullest and went to buy myself a cup of tea. I had not eaten anything since morning.

It might take another twelve hours to reach Pune." I thought for a second and went to buy some magazines. I knew it would be a long night and I would not get another sleep as I had just woken up. I had needed something to kill the time. I came back to my compartment and order for my meal. By that time most of the people had started to have their dinner. I knew the moment they finished with dinner, they would like to go for sleep. I looked for someone with whom I could chat a little. All the neighbors near my seat were either senior citizens or much older than me. This is always the case with me. I have traveled in train many a time and most of the time I found myself surrounded with people much older to me. It is not that I hate older people but because unlike us, they would prefer to sleep after dinner and any disturbance would invite resentment especially if you are a student. Fortunately, I saw a boy of my age a few seats away from me. He must have been studying in Pune, I thought and went straight to him.

"Hi, I am Rahul." I introduced myself.

"Hey, I am Sivam." He replied and offers me to seat there.

"You are going to Pune." I asked to start the conversation.

"Yeah." He said folding the novel he was reading.

I saw it was "Rich Dad, Poor Dad".

"It is a great book." I said and he just smiled.

He must have been thinking that why am I bothering him but within few minutes he looked quite comfortable talking to me.

"So what do you do in Pune?" I asked him.

"I am doing my MBA there." He replied.

"Oh really, I am also doing my MBA in Kolkata." I said in excitement.

"So you are in which year." I continue.

"I am moving to second year now." He said.

"So why are you going to Pune." He asked.

"I am going to meet one of my friend in Pune who had met with an accident." I replied in a distress manner.

"Oh I am sorry. Is he alright?" He tried to console me.

"I do not know yaar. He was in ICU when I had boarded the train. I do not know how is he now."

I said and turn my head towards the window.

"Do not worry. He will be alright. What does he do in Pune." He said and offers me water to drink.

"He is doing his MBA from Pune University. Our batch mate." I said and tried to gulp down some Water.

"Really, which Hostel? What is his name? Even I am doing my MBA from Pune University." He asked the moment I mention Pune University.

"Rishi, I do not know which hostel." I answered.

"Rishi Raj?" His voice increased many fold.

"Yeah, how do you know him?" I asked hurriedly.

"What has happened to him? I stay in the same hostel. In fact we are good friends." He got nervous and held my hand.

"How is he now? How has this accident happen?" He asked in total disbelief.

"What a small world." I thought for a second.

"He tried to commit suicide by consuming the whole bottle of sleeping pills." I told him once I knew he was a friend of his.

"What????" He exclaimed in disbelief.

"What are you saying? I had met him last week when he came to drop me at the station. I was going home to attend my sister's wedding. He told me to bring lots of sweets." He replied and I could see his wet eyes.

"He seemed to be alright." He continued.

"Did you see any changes in him lately?" I tried to ask him.

"He was as usual, quite normal. He had told me that he had some fight with his girlfriend Pooja. But I do not think that could be a reason. There must be something more had happened in my absence." He said and kept on looking outside from the window.

We kept on our conversation for some time when we had been advised by fellow train mates to sleep. We promised to go directly to the hospital once we reached there. I went back to my seat.

My conversation with Shivam had given me a hint that Rishi had a very steady relationship with Pooja Mishra. Both of them had known each other for four years. Pooja had helped him immensely during the time when he had failed in his business and went into hibernation. She is an outgoing girl and in whatever interaction I had with her, she seemed to be a good girl. She was a bit ambitious and wanted to get everything in a short period of time. She had done her MBA and was working in Pune. Rishi had decided to go to Pune so that he could spend more time with her. He was very passionate about her. He had lost everything and was alive because he had her at his side.

"What if she had dumped her and that led to his taking such an extreme step." I thought.

We will be able to know the exact reason of his taking such a step only when he comes out of hospital safely. I prayed for him and went into the sleeping mode again.

WHEN RISHI SPOKES.........

$2$3th July,2002. 14.20 Hours we reached Pune. Three hours behind schedule arrival of train. It was better keeping in mind the number of hours train runs late in India. We have the largest number of trains in our country and biggest railway connectivity; still we have done nothing to make it run on time, leave apart, making it the safest and cleanest form of mode of transport.

Shivam and I had decided to move directly towards the hospital. We got down from the train, stretched our body to the fullest and move towards the hospital in a cab. Having Shivam with me helped me in not asking the directions from anybody. In next forty minutes, we reached city hospital and ran towards the reception.

"Rishi Raj. Which room?" I asked as soon as I reached near the reception.

"Let me check sir." A middle-aged lady replied.

"Room number 302." She replied.

"It's on third floor sir. Please go to your right and take a lift." She explained.

"Thanks!!!"

I said and ran towards the lift. Shivam followed me.

As soon as I reached in room number 302, I saw Rishi sleeping on the bed. I went near him and stood there. The bottle hanging above him and syringe neatly pierced through the veins of his right hand. He was lying unconscious. His face had become a little darker. Perhaps, the after effects of poison, I thought. No one was present in the room except him. Before I reacted, Asad and one more guy entered into the room.

"Hey man, so good to see you." Asad hugged me the moment he entered.

"How is he?" I asked without wasting any time.

"He is out of danger now. Poison has been removed and he will be alright within some days." He replied.

"Hey shivam, how come you are here? When did you come back"? Asad asked the moment he saw Shivam.

"I met with Rahul in the train while returning and came to know about this." He said.

"When did this happen? He was absolutely all right before I left." He reasoned.

"Come let us go towards the canteen. We will talk there." Asad said and we moved out of the room.

"By the way, this is Ritesh. I hope you know him Shivam." Asad introduced Ritesh.

"He actually informed me about all this happening."

He actually went to his room to ask for some notes. When he did not open the room even after several attempts, he informed the warden.

"I first thought he must be sleeping. But I found the light on and music was also on. I tried hard to open the door. I tried to knock the door as hard as it could, but he did not respond." Ritesh mediated.

"I immediately called the warden and he broke open the door. The moment we entered, he was lying on the floor with fag coming out of his mouth. We immediately shifted him to here." He explained the whole story.

"Where is Pooja? I asked surprisingly when I could not find her.

"I tried to call her. She did not receive my call." Asad replied.

"I even tried to call Shally, her flatmate, but he even didn't pick up the phone." He continued.

"God, how could she is not be present?"

"There must be something wrong." I guessed.

"Even we are quite surprised that not only Pooja but Shally also never bothered to call me." Asad said surprisingly

My brain started relating something. It has to do something with them. Bloody, how could they are not present at this crisis. I had to find the truth.

"Did you find something wrong between Rishi and Pooja?" I quizzed Asad.

"Don't know rahul, I could not meet him lately as I was quite busy with our end sem exam." He said.

"Why? Why did you ask that?" He surprised.

"I believe, there must be something wrong. Look, at least Pooja would have been here at this time of crisis. She and Rishi have been in a relationship for quite a long time. I am really surprised with her absence." I said patiently.

They tried to be in consonant with me.

"Let's go to the room. He might be awake by now." I said and we moved towards his room.

"She has betrayed me. She is a bitch. Bloody!She is a fucking whore." Rishi shouted the moment he saw me.

"Hi buddy, take it easy. How are you? Whom are you talking about." I tried to console him.

He kept silent. I didn't try to intervene further and sat near him in a stool.

"Don't worry man. Everything will be fine." I said holding his left hand.

"Nothing would be same Rahul. She has devastated my world." He replied and I could see the pain in his voice.

"Our anticipation was coming right. It has to do with Pooja." I thought.

After a few minutes, he narrated the whole story.

That morning Rishi left his flat to attend the regular classes. Shally had already left for the institute. He was in his batch. They had known each other since the time they met in college and became good friends. They had taken a flat near the campus and was sharing it. I had also met with Shally once when I had visited them last. He seemed to be a smart chap. He hailed from Delhi and his father was a businessperson. He used to live his life quite recklessly. In a nutshell, I did not like his extravagant lifestyle. I had warned Rishi when he had decided to live with him. That day, Rishi felt a bit of uneasiness and decided to return home to take rest. The moment he enter the room, he saw Pooja embraced in the arms of Shally. She was in her bra and panties only. Her clothes were lying on the floor. Shally, in his undergarments, was patiently kissing all over her body. One hand of his was inside her panty and another holding her tightly with his body. They were so much engrossed in the act that they could not realize someone had entered the house.

You bastard." He shouted in a loud voice punching the table on the side. The ink bottle tumble down from the table and burst in a second.

"What the fuck you are doing." He exclaimed and went near them.

They were dumbfounded and separated from each other like an squirrel jumps onto the tree.

They had been caught red handedly.

"Rishi." She somehow managed to utter a word.

"Just a moment man. I tell you." Shally tried to intervene.

"You bastard, keep quite. I will talk to you later." He shouted in anger pointing towards shally.

"You bitch. How long has this been going on." I went wild.

My eyes welled up. I yelled at her. I held her tightly with both my hands and roared like a lion.

Why the fuck you did it.

You are making out with this fucker.

Leave me Rishi. It hurting me." she tried to move away from me and went to collect her clothes.

You have to answer me." I stuttered and stammered.

Shally kept on standing like that and gradually wore his pant.

His anger was increasing with their silence.

"I want the answer right now Pooja. Why did you did this? We have been in a relationship for so long. Why did you break my trust." He asked patiently.

"You will not understand Rishi." She said and went towards the door.

"What will I not understand damn it." He shouted and pulled her towards him.

"What will I not understand?"

"I will not understand what I have just seen or I will not understand all the bullshit that you people have been doing behind me or I will not understand how much I trust you people. Tell me what else you want me to understand." He was going ballistic with every passing second.

"Bloody! I will not understand that you are sleeping around with this fucker or I don't know with whom else." He roared fisting his boot on the floor many times.

"Mind your language Rishi. You have said enough. I do not know what you have been shouting."

She roared back.

"Yes, I have been sleeping around with him. Yes I have broken your trust. But what have you done."

"Tell me the last time that we had spent some quality time together. You have no time for me.

Tell me the last time that you have touched me, caressed me. You won't be able to remember.

Bloody you have been busy with your classes and those stupid kids of yours. Your priorities have changed since the time you had come here. I have become a piece of doll for you. Have you ever wondered what I want from you." She said in a breath.

"I never thought that you would ever behave like that. Bloody you are trying to say that our relationship was nothing except physical relationship. You would sleep around with anyone if I m not here. You bloody whore." He had crossed all the line.

"I don't know. I…I just fucking don't know." She stammered.

"If I was not good enough, if you were bored from me, you should have just told me. Why the fuck you are doing it behind me. Why is this crap….bullshit….i ….i bloody believed you so much." He reasoned

"Whatever you think. I was just…….just frustrated from you Rishi." He wailed.

"What? You were frustrated so you slept with him……"his anger had no bound.

"That's it Pooja. It is all over between us. I bloody do not want to see your face again. Do not ever come to me." He shouted and moved out of the room in a hurry.

He wept like a kid. We kept on listening to him silently.

I had come to know the truth. The girl he had loved all through his life had betrayed him and left him in a lurch. I would not be able to know the other side of story but one thing was sure, he has been devastated from all this happening. The mere involvement of him with an NGO in Pune had left him with no time for Pooja. Whatever time he has after the class, he used to spend it towards teaching the poor and orphanage from the NGO. He had never thought that his involvement with this noble cause would eventually snatch his only love in the world.

PRIYESH CALLED ONE DAY!!!

"Hello Rahul, can you hear me? I got a call from Priyesh one day.

"Yes Priyesh, I can hear you. Tell me how are you?" I asked in a jest.

Before I could hear something else the phone got disconnected. It was raining cats and dogs and the phone lines were not working.

We had almost negligible contact with him after what had happened on the farewell night. I had a few conversations with him after I had moved to Kolkata. He repents on what had happened that night but things had gone out of control. It had put the whole relationships amongst us in danger. He told me how bad he had feeling and had promised that one day he would make amend of his mistake. I had advised him to take time as it would somewhat heal the pain his mistake has created among the group. He had promised me that he would do everything.

141

The phone rang again.

"Hello Priyesh, yes tell me. I can hear you." I said in a jiffy.

"Yes Rahul, I have just called to say that I have been selected to Indian Institute of Management for two years MBA program."

I was speechless for a second.

"Wow!!" I exclaimed as it was a great news for me.

"I knew it Priyesh. I knew that if you use your brain in right direction you could do wonders." I said.

"I am very happy for you brother."

"I knew Rahul, you would be the first person who would be very happy to hear this."

"I want to call Ruchika also, Rahul." He said and I thought for a few seconds.

"I want to tell her how sorry I have been feeling for what had happened between us. I really mean it man.' He continued and I felt a kind of repentance in him.

"I have been the cause of a lot of suffering for my friends. I had vowed not to repeat the mistakes and prove to you all that I am worth it. I have been waiting for this day for ages Rahul." He was crying over the phone.

"We are not angry with you Priyesh. Whatever happened was not right but it all happened in the past. The important thing is that you have realized your mistake and want to rectify it. I know Ruchika would not mind talking to you. Afterall you people have been a very good friends and it all happened between friends. You have accepted the mistake and I believe this is what matter at the end." I replied and told him to call her at some point of time.

"But it has been over a year man. Would she accept my apology." He asked.

"It is never too late to accept your mistake, Priyesh. The important point is you are really sorry. I do not feel she would not accept it." I reasoned.

He disconnected the phone and promised me to call her and Asad and apologize for whatever he had done that day.

I felt so happy for him. He was a changed man. I could understand the kind of pain he had undergone to come so far. He had got the realization that life was not just all the fun. It has some value attached to it. Whatever may be the worth of his father, he had to prove himself at some point of time. He had been lived in the shadow of his father all through his days of upbringing and thus needed a true realization of his life which he had got with whatever happened with him in the last few years.

TIME CHANGES IN MINUTES!!!

It was the month of October. The month of Durga Puja celebration. We had returned from our summer training and eagerly waiting for these festivities. I have been away from Pia for almost two months when we were in different places for our summer internship. We had planned a great time during the festival and thus eagerly waiting for the festival to start. Unlike other parts of the country, durga puja is celebrated in Bengal for ten days. This is one festival when whole of Bengal is on a holiday mood and eagerly waits for the occasion. I had been very happy for many reasons.

First and foremost, I would be celebrating the festival with the girl I always wanted to have with me and secondly because of the success that Priyesh had got. This has not only made him believe in himself but more to what it had brought with it. He had called Ruchika a few days back and it seemed everything is normal between them. It has filled a big void that has been created that night.

I had planned a big surprise for her. I had borrowed my friend's bike as she loved bike ride. I wanted to take her for a long drive and rode her across the length and breadth of the city and enjoy the celebration. It would have been so nice to have a candle light dinner at a nice restaurant at the end. I had planned everything and just waiting for the time to come when I would take my lady love across the town over a bike.

With the start of a beautiful evening, I reached her hostel. She came out wearing a red suit. The hair flowing freely across the face and she looked absolutely elegant. She came near me and sat silently onto the bike and I pressed the accelerator and vroomed for an exciting journey. I took her across the salt lake. The evening breeze had added an absolute charm to the already pleasant weather. The evening had soon engulfed into a beautiful night. We reached park street and from there to esplanade. We stayed there for a few minutes and had gol gappa. The night sky looked magnificent with the arrival of thousands stars. The moonlight was giving everything a silver glow. The already decorated streets of Kolkata with lighting across the buildings make it absolutely brilliant. In this beauty I found her a little disturbed. She had not been speaking so much. The usual happiness around her face was missing. I tried asking her what's that bothering her but she declined with a sweet smile. I knew there is something back of her mind which is troubling her. I thought perhaps she must be missing her family as she was away from them for the first time on this festival. I tried my best to keep her in best frame of mind and enjoy the moment.

"Hey you know, I had fallen in love the moment I saw you at the college laboratory." I said, Casually, while roaming on the street of esplanade.

"Oh really, but I didn't feel that you were interested in girls. You used to look very shy." She replied.

"Yeah I was. But really I knew that this is the girl I want to live my life with. I was crazy about you, trust me." I saw her smiled a bit and I felt better.

It was all so romantic. Strolling down the lane of esplanade with a girl I really love so much. We had a nice dinner afterwards and we moved back to her hostel before the schedule time of return at the hostel.

Next morning was a holiday. I woke up well past nine that day. I had my breakfast at the hostel canteen. The hostel was almost empty as people had gone home for celebration. We had stayed back in Kolkata to witness the Puja there. I dwelled on the events of last night. I felt that she was not at all comfortable. I thought there was something bothering her. I wanted to know what had causing her such disappointment but could not be able to do that. She didn't tell anything even if I asked her many a times. I thought that time would heal that and thus involved myself with the flow of life post Puja celebrations.

It all went too far when she suddenly decided to go home at the beginning of her third semester exam. I did whatever I could to know what had made her leave everything in between and return home but could not be able to know the truth. She just told that she would be come back soon and appeared in re-exam and cleared her semester. She just said that her family is in some sort of problem and they need her. I didn't oppose her return and felt that there must be something which she would not like to share and thus would be alright soon. It all seemed dangerous when she called me that day and looked quite disturbed and in pain.

LIFE WITHOUT HER!!!

The sudden brake of the train awakens me. I peeped from the window of the train. We had reached Howrah Station. I looked at the upper birth but did not find Pia. We had always travelled together when we had moved to Kolkata. I missed the way she used to wake me up from a distance when train approaches to Station. I did not want to get down from the station. I remember feeling afraid from getting down. It was the fear that I had never known. It was a sinking feeling deep down from bottom of my body. I remember my feet were not moving and I was still lying on the birth and watching people grappling to get down.

"Bhaiya, station had come. You have any bags?" I heard one labour asking me if I had stuffs which he could carry.

I did not reply and slowly tried to move my feet out of the train. I walked towards the door and looked outside. There were heavy rush for people trying to move out of the station. I stopped at the door for some time when someone told me to move.

The moment I got down to Howrah station, It felt strange. It felt like I have come down to a strange place. Nothing seemed familiar to me. The station, the people, the place all looked so strange to me. I did not know which way to move. I remember her calling out loudly to the kully and directing them to collect our baggage. She had never let me carry the heavy luggage. I felt the absence of that care. I remember how she used to give five rupees extra to the person behind my eyes. I remember her gentle smile when I used to catch her giving those five rupees.

I often ask why she does that when we are paying them the exact wages. She would just smile and say" jane do na, they work so hard". I was just missing her holding my hand and coming out of the Howrah station. I had been missing every moment of her presence. I did not know what had happened to me. I was really terrified to come out of the station. I saw my heart was beating fast and I was sweating profusely. It was really incomprehensible at all. I went towards a bench and sat over it for a moment. I was trying to speak with me. One part of me was saying to come out of the station and start my life afresh while the other part was stopping me to do that. I closed my eyes and put my hands over it to wipe the tears that was started to come by than. I went to nearby tap and washed my eyes over and over again. I kept repeating to myself that this is not the end of life and I have to move but I really do not know was stopping me. I was helpless. I kept on sitting there for about twenty minutes when I decided to come out of the station. With that heavy heart I finally walked out of the station and booked a cab to my hostel.

One week had passed since I returned to Kolkata. I had not come to terms with my life. Life had been very tough. With her, everything else had gone. I missed the days when I had to complete the class and rush to catch a bus to Park street. We usually met there. Sometimes, I had to miss those extra classes to be with her. I would not let even a single day to pass without meeting her. I was missing all those days. It's been almost two weeks and I have not heard anything about her. Every day after class, I immediately go to the computer lab and first thing I do is to send her an email and keep on waiting the next day that she had replied. On every mail I wrote how much I loved her and how hard it was to live without her. I used to write to her about every moment that we had spent together. I had read and re-read all the letters and emails that she had exchanged while we were together. All those memories had only made me miss her more. With every passing second I was feeling a kind of void in my life. It was like I was dead from inside and was not interested in doing anything. The same books looked so unfamiliar to me. The buildings, the people and environment all seemed pointless to me. I was not the one I used to be. I tried very hard to feel the kind of passion I had when I joined this college and pushed myself very hard to become the person I used to be but failed miserably. I decided to pack my stuffs and go back home and tell my dad that your son has not only failed in studies but failed in life too. With that heavy heart I went to my room and started to collect my stuffs when someone knocked at my door and I turned to check.

"Hey, how are you? What happened, you are not coming to the class regularly?"

I saw Shreya standing in front of the door.

"Hey, yeah was not feeling well." I said in a very distressed voice.

"I know you must be missing Pia. But it is a matter of few days. She will be back soon." She Replied, not knowing that she has gone and would not return.

I had not told her that Pia had gone and would not return to Kolkata.

"She will not return and I am also going back to Ranchi leaving behind everything." I replied and looked at her in dismay.

She was dumbfounded.

"Whaaaaaaat? What the hell are you saying?" She was absolutely taken aback.

I narrated the whole story to her and she just could not believe what I had told.

"Did you receive any mail from he?." She asked immediately.

"No", I said and kept mum.

"Why don't you call her? she asked unaware of the fact that I had no contact number of her.

"I don't have her number. She had not given any contact details." I said and turning my head towards her"

"Why did she do it Shreya." I asked and stop there for a second.

"I don't know Rahul. She must be in some trouble. I just know that she loves you very much and she would definitely contact you.' She said and we moved out and sat on the pavement in our campus close to my hostel.

"You know Rahul, you should keep faith in God. I know how hard it is for you but I believe this is the time when you have to be very strong." She said.

"This is not the time to go back and leave everything behind. You have worked so hard to come so far. Think about the time when you must be working day in and day out to achieve this. Now when everything seems possible, you are thinking of leaving it." She was saying and I was just listening to her.

"Do you think Pia would have been very happy to know that you had left everything and wasted your life." She continued.

"But, Shreya, I am just could not able to concentrate on anything. I did try to regroup myself and pushed very hard to come to terms with it but failed miserably. I am just finished."

"You are not finished, Rahul. You think that you are finished. You are not able to take your mind off her. Think about your parents who are waiting for his son to become something in life. Think if Pia returns and sees you as a wasted man. Would she be happy to see you?

Never, she would never be happy for you."

"Have you seen yourself? You are not in your usual self. You are the shadow of the person you once were. Look at your face. You hardly smile and mingle with people that you used to do. You seemed like a person lost the battle of life." She said and I felt a kind of Pia in her. She used to tell me in the same manner when I was down.

"I am ok Shreya. It just that I do not like doing anything." I murmured and looked towards her.

"Just try to take your mind off her for some time. Be the person you were. Things would improve. I know what you have been going through. But this is not the end Rahul." She seemed to be concerned about me.

I felt good. I had someone who understands my pain and cares about me.

"Thank you Shreya. I really owe a lot to you. You have always been a help to me." I said and moved back to our hostels.

Time was passing in a hurry. I was trying to cope without her presence around me. The days had become a little more bearable. Shreya had been a constant source of support during this trial days. She had been trying to help me in every possible ways. What really helped was that I had started to concentrate more on remaining classes. Plus, in view of the approaching placement season, the placement team had started a two weeks personality development or PD class as we used to say. During these classes, they used to teach us how to face the job interview. What are the preparation require to appear for those job interview and things like that. Those extra PD classes had helped me to take my mind off her. A little though. Rest of the time, I had the company of Shreya and she made sure that I could enjoy my life and come out of this. Things have been started to improve and I had been moving on in life without her.

SHE FINALLY REPLIED.......

It had been over two months and I had not heard anything from her. During these two months, I had sent her innumerable emails asking about her whereabouts. I had contacted everyone; she could have possibly contacted and had got the negative response from all of them. By that time, I had learnt to live without her but every passing day I used to prey for her safety and security. I had the feeling that one day she would return and we would meet again. Life had been going on and I had been trying to involve myself in the preparation of placement season.

Shreya had been a great help to me. Over the last two months, she had become an important part of my life. She had taken care of me, like only Pia could have done at this important juncture of my life. I was in a great pain when I had returned to Kolkata. I did not know how I would survive without her. I was in total mess and could have easily been lost in the past had she not helped me and cared for me in those difficult time. She had made sure that I attend the remaining classes and if in case I could not, she as usual made my proxy. She had been doing that for long now.

"Did you fill the placement form?" she asked me one day while we were having our usual evening walk after diner.

"Yeah. I did that".

"So, how is your PD class going on?"

"It's been great so far. They have been trying to mould our self into the nitty gritties of interview process." I replied.

So, in a few days we will be leaving this place and move to a new destination." She said turned her head towards me.

"It feels so nostalgic even now." She continues.

"Hmmn, yes."

We kept mum for a few seconds when she broke the silence.

"Will you miss me." she said and I could see a tinge of sadness in her face.

"Of course," I uttered and stopped for a moment.

I will not be able to forgive you Shreya. After Pia had gone, you had stood with me like a rock.

You have brought me back to where I had left. My life had become a vaccum since she had gone away. You have filled that vaccum. I had almost lost in her absence but you have reignited the fire in me. I would not be able to forget you even if I try to.

She remained silent for a while.

"So none could replace Pia in your life Rahul." She said and looked at me.

I was numb. I knew what she wanted to ask. I had been feeling in her a kind of likeness for me.

For past few weeks, we had been spending a lot of time together and in those times she had almost made me forget Pia. But she had asked something which I could not do at least in this birth. I may have been trying to live without Pia but it would have been almost impossible to replace her with anyone else. She had been in my every breadth. Falling in love again was absolutely out of question with me. Shreya was a great girl and had I not been in a relationship, I would not hesitate for a second to fall in love with her. she was one of the best friends that I had made over the years and thus I did not want to hurt her.

"I do not know Shreya. I do not know if Pia would return and I would forget her." I could say only that.

"It is ok Rahul. I just asked." She replied and we moved towards our hostel.

She had not asked that question in general. She had meant it and I know what she must have been going through. I always knew she had been falling for me. her question kept on revolving around me and I felt a kind of dizziness and thus went towards my room. I fall flat on my bed and kept my eyes closed. In a few minutes, I got up and generally went to turn my computer on. I had not done this for many days. The moment I opened my rediffmail account, I could not believe my eyes. I had got a reply mail from Pia. Within a few seconds I quickly pressed the key to open the mail.

She had wrote,

Dear Rahul,

I know you must have been very angry with me. My mailbox is flooded with you mails and I have not replied any of your mail. I could not even say sorry as I know how much you have been suffering because of me. Since the time I have come heer, there is no moment where I have not missed you. Many a times, I thought of running away from here and go to you. But every time, my priorities have stopped me from doing so. I am still not in a position to tell you anything. I know you must be preparing hard for your placement. You would be very happy had I were present there. But this could not had to happen. Fate has brought me farthest from you. You would be surprised to see as why I am writing to you now. Why not I tried to contact you before? You will have a number of questions but I could not answer any at the moment. I have just come to tell you that the moment had arrived for which you had been strive so hard. I knew you must have been trying very hard for the placement. I know, my Rahul, would not disappoint me and would get the best plac ement in the history of the institute. So best of luck!!!

Love

Pia

NEW BEGINNINGS!!!!

Last six months of my stay in Kolkata was hell of a time. I had to deal with the absence of Pia on one hand and on the other prepares well for the forthcoming placement season. One way I was in great distress of possibility to lose Pia forever and on the other had hope for a better beginning to my career for which I had worked so hard. I had to grab the other opportunity as in that way I would be able to keep the promise that I had given to Pia, to take care of my life and do well in all my endeavors in her absence. One good thing that I had was the presence of Shreya, who had by than become an integral part of my life. We had come closer and she almost helped me out in all my work. I would not have been able to complete my study had she was not with me in those terrible time of my life. She stood with me like a pillar of strength.

When placement season ended, I had been selected for one of the fastest growing FMCG Company in Mumbai. Shreya had been selected for a multinational bank and had to move to New Delhi.

On our farewell night,

"So in a week's time we would be leaving Kolkata." Shreya asked me as I was sipping my glass of beer.

"Yeah, it's the beginning of a new journey." I said casually and looked at her.

"And I would not be with you in this journey," she replied and I saw her looking at me quite intently.

She was almost in tears.

"Hey, what happened, Shreya" I had never seen her so quiet.

"Distance would not keep us apart." I said and held her hand, keeping my beer glass on the table.

"You know what, it is because of you that I am been here." I said and looked at her eyes.

"I would not be able to forget you Shreya. You have been so kind to me." I continue.

"Then why are you going Rahul?"

"Can't we stay together? I would not be able to live without you." I had never thought she would ever tell me this.

I remained silent for a while.

"I am sorry Rahul. but I had a feeling for you. I would be in trouble had I not tell you what I feel for you." She was telling me and I kept on looking at her.

"I know you loved Pia so much. But in these few months I could not control to fall for you." She continues.

"I know how difficult it is for you to forget her. I also know you might not be thinking in the same way. But I could not control myself to Rahul." she stopped.

"I am sorry Shreya. It is so difficult for me now to think beyond her. you are the only girl other then Pia with whom I had come so close. We have spent many memorable days. But I am not in a position to forget her." I replied and move closer to her.

The sound of music had gather the high volume by that time and most of people had involved in some great dancing act.

"You are such a sweet heart Shreya. But try to understand me." I held her hand tightly.

She was in tears and I was not feeling well either.

"I know Rahul. It's not gonna happen. You must be thinking that I am a fool." She tried to wipe her tears.

"Would you keep in touch with me." she tried to hide her tears and I saw a cute smile appear on her face.

"No", I tried to tease her.

"I would kill you if you do not send me a mail daily or call me." she made a guerrilla face".

"Hahaha, you are a darling. I would not be able to forget you." I said and hugged her.

"Oh yes, I have something for you." She said and turned towards her bag.

I saw her getting out one properly wrapped box and hand over to me.

"What is this?" I asked her.

"Nothing, it would not let you forget me." she said

"And yes, do not open it until we have left Kolkata." She warned me and we moved towards the dance floor.

Two days later she packed her baggage and moved to New Delhi. Next morning I boarded the train back to my home town. I had entire month before I could start my job.

By that time most colleges had their placement season over. Asad and Namit had already reached Ranchi and we had planned a big get together. Ruchika and Ravi arrived a few days later.

Asad had been placed with an FMCG major in Dubai. He had entire two months to go there and start the job. Namit had been placed with a consumer durable company in Pune. Ruchika had to go to New Delhi to join a bank and Ravi was joining an investment banking in Chennai. Rishi had left his management in last semester after that incident and had formed an NGO Growwell and had working there full time. We had a reunion of sorts in Ranchi before we could again move for what we believe a new beginning in our life!!!

LIFE 8FTER!!!!

We had a great reunion. What made it even more special was presence of Priyesh. He had come all the way from Bangalore. It would have been perfect reunion had Pia also joined us. In a few days later we all moved to our respective destination. I was the last one to leave. I was going to a place which was not new to me. I had some of the best ever moments of my life there. The moment I got down to Mumbai Station, I felt a kind of zeal. I had dreams in my eyes and hopes in my heart for the beginning of an important chapter of my life. For the first time, I had not been thinking about any other thing than making a life out of nothing. While unpacking my baggage, I found the box given by Shreya. It had been over a month that we had been separated and in last one month I had sent her a few mails and called her a few times. She had been busy with her banking job. When I opened the box, I found a beautiful picture of her which I had taken in college. She looked gorgeous as ever. I gently kept the frame on a stool besides my bed. Next morning, I got up quite early. I wore a new suit with a matching tie which my father had gifted me while leaving for Mumbai. I got out of the house and caught a taxi to go to Nariman Point where our company had its headquarter. The city didn't seem alien to me.

I had been here before. Only difference was, this time Pia was not with me. After running for an hour I reached Nariman Point and went straight to the reception of the building. I entered into the place which is going to be shaping my destiny.

We were six people from different colleges. Four boys and two girls. We were called in a conference room and like any other company, HR people did some formalities. We were told about the company and department where we had to work. It went on till evening with some introductory lectures from head of departments. While returning, I went to nearby cyber café to check my mails. I had not been able to do that in last few days. As soon as I opened the mail box, I found a number of mails from almost everyone. But none from Pia, as usual. One by one, I kept on reading the mails. Shreya had wrote about her experience in first few days of work.

She had been running across different vertical in the company. At the moment she had been with the credit card division. Asad had recently joined in Dubai and was almost lost in the beauty of the place. Other then his work, he had written everything about the place. He had been quite impressed with the beauty and availability of basic infrastructure of Dubai. In a few days only, he had been comparing them with that of India. Ravi had just written that he had joined the bank and is moved to Chennai. Ruchika as usual, was very happy with whatever work she had been assigned. I was quite disturbed to read about Namit. He had been traveling across Bihar and UP. Almost everyday, he had to travel somewhere remote. He had been assigned with rural sales.

A few days went on like that. We had been staying in the company provided accommodation.

We had to vacate the place in a month times and before that I had to find a place in Mumbai and make it my home. Daily after work, I had to visit a number of property dealers to find a suitable accommodation. This is the most difficult part of our stay in Mumbai. It is said that, you can get everything in Mumbai except the roof above your head. This is so true. One night, as soon as I returned to my room, I got a call from reception that I had a call from Delhi. I knew it could be no one except Shreya. I had not contacted her in almost a week.

"Hello," I said the moment call passed on to my receiver.

"Hey, how are you, my dear?" It was shreya

"So you had forgotton your promise." She said before I could responded.

"Ahh…actually".

"I know, you would say that you are very busy with your work." She replied before I could answer.

"Yes, I mean no...not busy with the work but in finding a place in Mumbai." I finally responded.

"I had to vacate the hotel soon and need an accommodation as soon as possible." I continued.

"Oh, so my baby is house hunting." She had used the word for first time.

"Any progress?"

"Nope, still the same situation."

"Oh baby, don't worry. You would get one soon." She replied.

"I hope so..."

"You will. Ok tell me did you open my gift?" She had asked after almost a month.

"Yeah, it's beautiful. You look gorgeous."

First time ever I had used such adjectives for her. It is not that she was not beautiful before. But I had never seen her like that before. I was constantly thinking of Pia. I was unable to see anything beyond her.

"Wow!!" She exclaimed like a little girl.

Yeah, its true. You always were but...."

"But what, dear?".

"I don't know...."

I didn't know what was happening to me. I had never talked to her like that. Was am falling in love again? I really didn't know.

Only thing I knew was I really loved Pia a lot and would always wait for her.

OF NAMIT'S WOES.....

Three months have passed since we had joined our respective organizations. Most of us were in different cities. We had been trying to cope with the changes that had been coming with each passing day. In last three months, we had little interaction with one another. We used to speak once in a while over mobile phone which had by now gradually included in our fetish. Usually, we had been in constant touch over e-mail. The cheapest and easiest way of communication at that point of time. Moreover, we could express our feelings better which we could not do over phone as it would have cost us a lot of our hard earn money. I made sure to write an email to each one of my group every week and in most cases got their reply. I keep on writing to Pia as well but as usual could not get reply. One fine day, while checking my mails first thing in the morning, I found a mail from Namit. He had been transferred to look after the territory of Bihar.

He was with a consumer durable company. In last three months, he had been transferred to three different states. He had started it from Maharastra, moved to Utter Pradesh and now shifted to Bihar. He had not been constant in one place. He had written how difficult his life had been. The moment he unpacked his stuffs, he had been told to move to a different territory.

Life had not been good to him of late. Other then professional front, he had been struggling to keep his relationship with Ria in tact. He had not been able to keep constant touch with her. He was into hard core sales teams and had to meet certain target every month. Most of the times, he was in some interior areas of the state. The pressure of intense traveling across the states has also affecting his health. Moreover, he had the extreme pressure to perform every month and achieve the given target. He had written about his altercation with Ria which had been increasing with every passing days. He was not able to speak to her for weeks and most of the times when he speaks with her, it always ends in some kind of altercation. Ria belongs to a conservative family and thus her father wanted her to get married and settle down. They have been looking for an ideal match for her. Most of the times, she used to tell him to settle down at one place and think about marriage. Namit was not in that state to think of getting married and thus the situation was going from bad to worse. He was not able to concentrate well in his personal as well as professional life.

I could not sleep well that night. I kept on thinking that in a few months life has become so difficult. Just a few months back, we had been living our lives out of all these difficulties. We had been working day in and day out to get to where we are today. We used to think that the moment we came out of our college life and moved into the professional one, every difficulty would be over and we would lead a peaceful life. We would be earning what we used to call our own money and would not hesitate and keep our desires inside us. We would be able to do everything that we have desired all these years. We did not know that life would become so hectic and we would not have the time to do all things that we wanted to do. We would not have the same friends with whom we have spent the most important days of our lives. Few years back, we were together. We had overcome so many difficulties. Now, if a friend was in pain we had no time to go and share his pain. It is like we had been clutched in a chain and could not move out of our own will. We had lost our independence.

Over a few weeks we exchanged a number of emails. Every time I told him to be a bit patient and keep on talking to Ria. The only way he could make his relationship better by having regular conversation with her. I had gone through the same pain and anxiety. I knew how difficult it would be for him to focus on the job in hand. He would be at least better as he could actually talk to her and discuss the matter. I did not have that luxury. I did not even know what had been going through her life. How is she coping up without me? What could be the reason for her not contacting me? I did not even know if she would ever remember me.

For the next few weeks, I could not make contact with Namit. I had been sent to southern part of the country on a promotional tour. I was away from Mumbai for almost a month. I was constantly moving to the southern regions and was not that regular with emails either. Ruchika called me the day I returned to Mumbai after my assignment,

"Hey, how are you Rahul. Long time. Where have you been all these days?"she asked me the moment I received the phone.

"Hey, was traveling to south India for an assignment. You tell me." I replied.

"Job as usual. I am planning a trip to US to meet Rakesh." She replied and stopped.

"Oh that's nice".

"Yup".

"Have you talked to Namit lately." She asked me abruptly.

"No, what happened? I asked as I felt she seemed a little concerned".

"Nothing, I had called him yesterday. He did not seem alright. He had left the job and is at home." She said and I recollected everything that we had discussed before I left for the tour.

"Really, did he tell anything? I could not able to speak to anyone since I went for the tour." I replied.

"No, he didn't tell anything but I believe he is in some kind of problem." She replied and we disconnected when I told her that I would find the reason and call her again.

"I immediately rang him at his mobile but it was switched off. I did try to call him a few times more but every time it has the same answer. I decided to wait for a few moments and rang him again and in every occasion I heard the same tune. I went inside to get his home number which I had wrote in my diary. Several attempts of mine to get connected with him had failed. I sent an email to him with the hope that he will reply once he checked it but even after a week I did not get any response from him. I did try to contact to Ria as well but did not get any satisfactory response except the fact that she had not talked to him for a month. With every passing day, my anxiety level increases to the maximum and I tried to contact whosoever could possibly provide me some information about him but my attempt failed miserably. None had any inkling of where the hell he was. Soon I found myself immersed in a project and went to Chennai. One night while checking my mails, I found a mail from Namit. With the flip of a second, I clicked on the mail. He had not written much except that he is fine and had given one number where he could be reached. Without wasting even a second, I dialed his number.

"Where the hell are you man?" I asked the moment he received the phone.

"For the last 2 months, I have tried to contact almost everyone who could provide me any information about you. But no one had any idea of your whereabouts. What the hell you are doing?" I continued in the same vain.

"I have sent you innumerable mails asking about you. You could at least reply once." Perhaps my frustrations were coming out of me in a jiffy.

"Hey, I am sorry yaar. It's just that I could not log in in last two months. Mobile was switched off and we had been to our native place." He replied in a sombre way.

"Everything is over man. I have shattered." He said and I could sense his pain.

"What happen buddy. Please tell me." I tried to calm him.

"Last time when I had spoke with you, I had told you about my relationship with Ria was going from bad to worse. I had been trying to make a balance with my professional and personal life.

One morning, I received a phone from my home. My father had a severe heart attack and I had to rush back home." He stopped in between.

"What? How is he now?" I sensed something terribly wrong.

"He is no more." He started crying like a child.

"Oh, fuck!". I had no words. I stopped for a few seconds.

I am so sorry yaar. You should have at least contacted us. You have suffered it alone. I didn't know how to react at that point of time. I did try to console him but I knew what he was undergoing at that moment.

"How is everyone at home. Is aunty alright?" I tried to change the topic.

"How is Ria? Did you get to talk to her," I was trying to ask possibly everything that could pull him back from that state.

"She has been married to someone in Dubai." He said and became silent.

"What? How?" I was speechless. How could she do that? Its just not fair.

"We had been advised to take my father to Kolkata. He was admitted there for almost fifteen days and he was recuperating well. Unfortunately, he got another heart attack and doctor could not save him. We went to our native place for his last rites and return only to hear that she had been married a few days before. I had met with her sister and she told me that she did try to contact me when her marriage was fixed. But since she could not get through to me, she had no option but to marry." He said.

"It is so unfortunate. I know how much you have suffered. I can feel your pain. Life has not been kind to you."

"What have you been thinking now. Are you planning to join back to work?" I asked casually.

"I have not reported to work for almost two months and had not informed the concerned authority regarding my absence. They have taken someone else on my place and I have lost my job as well."

I had absolutely no words which could explain my reaction at that moment. I could not even console him. He was in an intense pain and I could do nothing except listening to his sorrow over the phone. I had been talking to a man who over a few months lost his father, got the news of his girl friend married to someone else and lost his job. I kept the phone down and promised him to meet soon. For the rest of night, I could not sleep and kept on thinking about the man who had taught us to smile and be merry in any kind of adversity. Today that man has lost everything.

SOMETHING TO CELEBRATE!!!

The moment I entered into the office and went towards my cubical, I received a call from Mandy, my boss's secretary. Boss has called me into his chamber. I had returned last night from a month training programme on changing market dynamics and consumer behavior's pattern. I had no inclination as in why I had been summoned to his cabin at this hour. I have never been to his chamber as early as this hour ever in last one and half year except on a few occasions when we had our Monday morning meeting at his chamber. I didn't even get my laptop out of the bag and instantly moved towards his chamber.

I knocked at the door and entered when he called me in. I saw sumit, the chief strategy officer, also sitting in front of him. I gently pull the chair a bit and sat besides him as I have been told.

So how was the training module Mr. Rahul? He asked the moment I sat.

It was fantastic sir. I got to learn a lot from it." I said firmly and didn't move an inch from my chair.

"That's really great. So you would be wondering why we have called you so early." He said and I saw a little smile on his face.

It made me a bit relaxed as I knew there was nothing really serious as I had expected while going inside.

"Yes, I mean I just returned last night and thus had little knowledge as what has been going on here. Thus was a little apprehensive." I reply quite confidently.

"I hope you have not unpacked your stuffs, Rahul as you have to move again." He said and I raised my head towards him.

"Yes, you have been selected from this office to go to UK for six months intensive training programme as part of our young talent scheme." He said and handed over an envelope to me.

I was dumbstruck. I had never expected it at first place. I mean I knew about the programme and how many people across the globe been benefited from the scheme. I quickly took the envelope and tried to open it in a jiffy.

"You have all the time young man. You can read it when you go back to your desk. I hope you are happy and I think you deserved a little smile on your face." He politely said and moves his hand towards me.

"Thank you very much sir. I stood from my seat and gently move my hand to have a good shake hand.

"All the best young man, I know you would make us proud one day." He said and I quickly made an exit from the cabin.

While coming back, I could not believe my luck. I steadily returned to my cubical and in a hurry opened the envelope and read the contents in one go. I could not believe what has just happened to me. I mean, so many people really worked very hard to receive this and thus it makes me very proud that I am going to be the one. I raised both my hands in excitement and took a big breath. After all something great had happened to me in a long long time.

I saw Pundir standing behind me. He sat just opposite me and thus had come to know why I had been called in the boss cabin early in the morning. Actually, it has never been a good sign to be called in so early in the boss cabin and thus people were curious to know about the outcome of my meeting. He saw my excitement and thus could not stop himself in coming to me.

"I think, something good has happened." He said the moment I turned towards him.

"I gently gave him the letter.

"What, you have resigned or what. " he exclaimed with a wry smile.

I didn't utter a word and just kept on smiling.

"Congratulations….I mean it is just incredible." He just coudnt stop him.

His voiced was good enough to make the entire floor wondering what has happening there.

Soon many people gathered around my cubical.

"Man, this is just amazing. People, our dear friend Rahul has been selected for the young talent development programme and he soon going to UK." He has announced the news before I could react to it.

Soon the congratulation message poured over me like a sudden outburst of rain. It was like a hordes of people gathered around my cubical trying to hold my hand. I had been feeling like a celebrity with whom people wanted to shake hands and clicked a picture.

"It calls for a big celebration man." Pundir was ecstatic.

"Of course, it would be." I said and tried to take the letter from him. I didn't want it to be torn in this melee. I had been working day in and day out for this moment.

I wanted to go back home and hand this letter over to my dad and say that I have done it. He would be so happy to know that I have achieved something for which he had been waiting for days. Pia would be so happy to see this, I thought. It has been a long time that I had thought about her. The hectic schedule of mine has kept me out of all this for a long time. I didn't remember the last time I had thought about her. I could not stop myself to remember her at this time of celebration as she is the one who inspired me to do something out of my ordinary life and here I am celebrating the most successful day of my life, alone at my office cubical.

I could not concentrate on my work the whole day. The thought of my going to UK has not been sinking and I was constantly looking at the time when I go back home and dialed everyone and tell them about my achievement.

The moment I entered into my room, my phone rang and I saw Shreya calling.

"Hey, what a pleasant surprise. I was about to call you." I said in excitement.

"Wow! It's a pleasant surprise for me dear. How come you remembered me.?" She asked quite mysteriously.

"Actually she didn't expect such a reply. I had hardly called her in last two months when I was mostly away from Mumbai.

Yes, its true. Guess what, I have a very good news to share with you." I said quite happily.

"Hey, she is back or what?" I could sense her dwindling voice. I mean, she was the one who would be very happy for me if Pia had returned but we human beings rarely hide our emotion.

"I wish she were" I said quite melancholy.

"But it's not the case. I am really so happy to share with you that I have been selected for the young talent development program from India. I would be going to UK for six months as a training program".

I said in one breath.

"Oh my god, congraaaatulation!!!", I could see her enjoyment.

"I am so happy for you dear. You really deserved it". She exclaimed in pure happiness.

"I wish I were there to congratulate you personally." She said.

"I am so, so, so happy for you. I love you!!", Her happiness had no boundary.

I do not know what made me talking to her for a longer period of time. Next morning I mailed everyone in my group about my selection. In a few days I had to leave for a place I had never thought of in my life.

FATE HAD OTHER PLANS!!!

There was some time before I had to leave for London. Everything seemed to be working out perfectly. I had been doing the work that I always wanted to do. It would have been perfect, had Pia been there with me at this juncture of my life. My father was very happy with the prospects that one of his sons has been going to London for work. It has been really a proud moment for my family. They had been waiting for this day for a long time and when this has happened, they wanted to enjoy it. My father had booked his ticket and had wanted to travel to Mumbai to see me off at the airport.

I had invited a few of my office friends over to my home in Mumbai. This was a celebration for my selection for London. It has been a long time since I had such celebration. Since the time I had come to Mumbai, I hardly got time to enjoy. Most of the time I had been travelling or out of the city. Whenever I was in town I did not

185

feel like celebrating and thus used to be confined in the vicinity of my home. I had been living a life of reclusive. It was after almost a year of struggle, misery and agony that I had got this opportunity to be myself and enjoy the way I wanted to. It was a Saturday evening and thus the celebration continued till the wee hours.

Next morning I woke up with a heavy head. I had drunk a whole lot of whiskey last night and thus had a high. I went up to the refrigerator, got a cold water bottle and drank it in one breath.

I felt a bit better. I peeped outside the window. Being a Sunday morning, it was a bit deserted. I hope people had been enjoying an extended sleeping session. A few kids were playing in the society park though. For a few moments I stood there in silence and thought about my impending departure from here. It's been more than a year in Mumbai and I had never got this opportunity to peep outside my window and think about what had been going on in the society. I had met a selected few during my walking down and up from the stairs. This city looked as alien to me as I had come here for the first time. One week more and I would fly to a new destination. It would be going to be the same in London I believed.

The impending travel to London has filled in my senses. I was filled with a sense of impatience and urgency, like never before. I wanted to explore the city I had made my home for so many days.

I had decided that I would visit almost every place that I had heard of in next one week.

Next day I left office way before the usual time and the first place that I visited was marine drive. I went to the same place where Pia and I had so many memories. I sat on the same pavement where we had sat and I had embraced her in my arms. It had not changed at all.

I had been recollecting everything that we had discussed that day and almost sank in that feeling when a sudden rush of water after colliding with the boundary shook my entire senses.

For a few seconds I thought that Pia was with me and we had been enjoying a beautiful day at the serene environment of marine drive. I do not know why I thought that she is somewhere around and it was just a matter of time when she would be in my arms. With that feeling I took a cab and went towards Gateway. I had been doing exactly the same as we had done when we had come to Mumbai for the first time. The only difference was, this time she was not with me.

I spent a few hours at the gateway and decided to return home when I saw the time. It was ten minutes past five and I ran towards VT station to catch a local before it was getting crowded with people returning from offices.

It did not really matter when I entered VT station. It had already crowded with people running like crazy to catch their train back home. I took a cup of tea from the corner shop and moved towards the platform. Hordes of people kept rushing by me and I was making sure that the tea did not jump out of my hand in this frenzy. As I was enjoying a sip of my tea I saw someone zipped passed me like a hare jumped into the hole as it sees the cat. I could not believe what I had been seeing in front of my eyes. I had been watching the girl going away from me and I was not able to move my feet. I was freezed at the position. I kept in that posture a few moments when someone collided with me from behind throwing my cup of tea on the floor and tea droplets sprayed over my face. I raised my hand somehow pointing towards the girl and shouted in full sound.

Piaaaaaaaaaaaa!!!!

The train by then had left the station. I ran like crazy towards the train throwing whatever came in my way. The train started to keep pace and I was running behind it pointing towards the train that somebody please stop it. None could come in my rescue although I kept on running behind the train until it left the platform. I stood there in silent and kept on looking at the train until it disappeared from my eyes. It was not a dream. I had seen her at the station.

I looked around me and saw people staring at me and saying something in the local language. I did not blame them. They would never know what that train meant to me at that moment.

They would not understand the pain I had been undergoing. I did not know what to do, as I made my way home.

The moment kept on revolving around me. I had become restless. It felt like I had no power in my body and someone just carrying me to my home. I was feeling quite agitated with me. As soon as I reached home I fisted my hand on the table in frustration that I was not able to hold her. The more I thought about it, the angrier I became. The earlier peace that I had attained had quickly evaporated like the fragrance of a perfumed when it is left open. I kept on moving here and there in the room and the same feeling kept on revolving around me. Nothing seemed to have given me the peace that I had when I left home in the morning. God, she is in town but had not even tried to contact me. One part of me had trying to say that she could not contact me as she didn't know where I had been over the years while the other part was saying that she could have mailed me that she had returned to the country and living in this city. Nothing seemed to be giving me logical deduction of her absence. I had been losing my patience and thus I thought talking to Shreya would help.

I dialed her number but she didn't pick up.

I dialed again but no response. I banged my phone over the bed in frustration and sat on the chair keeping both my hand over the eyes. I was about to cry when the phone rang.

"Where the hell were you Shreya?" I asked the moment she picked up the phone.

She was aghast to hear this from me. I had never talked to her like that before.

"Hey, what happened dear. You seemed to be in trouble." She understood my anxiety.

"I had been calling you Shreya. You just could not believe what had just happened to me." I said.

"What ....what happened?" She just dragged the question.

"I just could not tell you. She was in front of me and I just could not hold her Shreya. She was so near to me. Bloody how could I do that." I was still frustrated with myself.

"Who was near you? I didn't understand what are you saying." She asked.

"Piaaa....", I said and kept mum.

"Whaaaaaaaaaaaaaaat? What are you saying?" She was as surprised as I had when I saw her.

"I really do not know what are you saying Rahul? How come she is here?"She asked.

She was here Shreya. I saw her.

"You must be mistaken. How could she be here in Mumbai." I could sense her depleting sound over the phone.

"She is in Mumbai, dear. I saw her catching a train."I replied.

"For a moment I thought, I had been day dreaming. I saw her zipping passed me in a hurry." I continued.

"I thought she had been coming towards me. I thought she would embrace me in a moment and say that I really missed you in all these days." I was putting so much emotion in every word.

"But that did not happen Shreya. She ran towards the Train and I kept on looking at her." I was saying and she just kept on listing to me.

"I didn't know what was going through her mind. I just didn't think anything beyond that. I know it would not go down well with her. But I cudnt stop myself in expressing my feelings with her.

I can understand Rahul. I know what you have been trying to say." She could only tell.

"Why had not she contacted me Shreya? Has she forotton me?" I questioned her.

She kept mum for a few seconds and then said.

"She would contact you Rahul. I know, she must have come lately and would contact you the moment she gets time."

"Would she need time to meet me Shreya? I have been waiting for her like ages and she does not have time to meet me. She would have contacted me the first thing while touching down here. I think something was not right.

I didn't sleep the whole night. The same picture kept on revolving around my mind for a long period of time. With every passing second, my impatience level kept on increasing. I wanted to go back to the station and wait in anticipation that she would come again and this time I would not let her go. I do not know when sun appeared and a new day begun.

There was a week left before I had to leave Mumbai. Everything seemed to have worked out perfectly for me in last few months. I have been getting recognition in my work place. I had been trying to live my life without Pia around and my friends have been by and now settled when this sudden turn of events had happened. I didn't know what to do and how to connect with her. I just had her email ID which I believe by now would have been flooded with my emails but had received no reply from her. I thought I should mail her and narrate her what I had seen last evening. The first thing I did when I reached office was to mail her and asked her why she had not contacted me yet. The moment I press the sent button, my brain kept on looking at the inbox at every passing second with the anticipation that she would definitely going to reply me this time. I kept on pressing the inbox every now and again that perhaps her mail had come and is not showing in the inbox. I checked the junk mail, spam mail and whatever mails were available but didn't receive any reply. I kept on looking at the clock. The impatient level kept on increasing and I was not able to concentrate on the work. I knew I had to go to the station and wait there in anticipation that if she were the regular travelers, she would certainly cross my path at the same time. With that anticipation I took my boss permission to leave early and moved towards the station.

I reached VT station way before five o clock and sat on the bench at the platform she had caught the train last night. My eyes were scanning every other girl passing through me. I didn't know what I had been doing and would not care what people might have been thinking. I didn't know what had going to happen to me if people caught me eye teasing and staring at every other girl. I had been just looking for her. The hours passed and there were no sign of her. I didn't move an inch. I kept on sitting there with anticipation that she would come. I saw a policemen coming near me. He came beside me and stood there for five minutes. He scanned me from down to up and asked what I have been doing there sitting idle and looking at every other women crossing. I told him I had been waiting for someone and she had been struck somewhere. He left the place only when he was satisfied that I had nothing suspicious with me.

I got up there and kept on moving here and there from one platform to other but she didn't turn up. It was already 10 pm when I decided to return home.

I continued this exercise for next two days. I took my boss permission and went straight to the station. I reached the station and sat on the bench and scanning the girls. I did try to move here and there in between in order to avoid the same cop come and asked me the same question.

Everything at the station was just the same. People running frenetically to catch the train and go home. I kept on looking for her and return home when did not find her again.

By the fourth day, when I went to my boss and asked his permission he called me inside his cabin.

"What is this Rahul, everyday at around 4 o clock you are leaving office and going somewhere? Is everything all right?" He asked me.

I kept mum for a second when he asked again.

"Tell me if you need something. I hope you are absolutely fine."

"It s just a matter of two more days and you will fly to London. I do not know but I have been observing a unique change in you." He continued.

"I know boss. I am perfectly all right. I just could not tell you what has been going on but I need to leave office by early." I said unmindful of the fact as how it would go down with him.

"Look Rahul, I know what you have been doing would be right, but I just sensed something wrong and thus asked you. If you feel you need some time I could extend your departure for a few days." he said.

"I would be perfectly all right sir. I would go to london as planned. It is just that I need some time before going out of her" I pleaded.

"All right. I know you very well. You can go." He said and I rushed out of cabin and moved out of the building in haste.

I had to go to the station.

If I tell someone why I have been visiting station and sitting there idly, they would have thought that I have gone out of my mind. They had absolutely unaware of my inner turmoil. I could not tell anyone what had been undergoing inside me. I reached station and frenetically started to search everyone. The police, people and other things around me were going about their usual business, just like before. But for me the world had stopped at one place. I was freeze at one point and had paralyzed with fright. As the time passed by, I broke into a cold sweat. I observed increase of heart beat and I was breathing fast. I knew I had to do something otherwise I would not be able to get her ever. I sat for ten minutes on the bench and tried to bring my mind in order. I kept on moving from one end of the platform to other to find a glimpse of her in case she comes. She didn't come and I kept on sitting there for long. I know I would not be able to meet her again. For me, it was the end of the world. Finally, in a daze, I made my way home thinking that would I be ever able to meet her again?

I DID MEET HER.....

I had to catch a flight on Saturday night. Tomorrow would be my last day in Mumbai before I leave for London. I had decided that I would stop my search for her and would not go to station again. I had given an excuse to my heart that I would be able to meet her if we were destined to meet. I didn't believe in this principle but I do not know why I had always followed this. I remember the time when I had proposed her and she had declined. I had left it on faith and it had worked for me. I decided that I would go to office and meet everyone and thank them for everything that they had done which had made my work easier. I would return home and would take my dad to dinner who had come from so far.

The moment I entered into the office, I had been called in the boss cabin. I knew it had to do with my impending departure and thus went inside.

"So young man, are you ready to fly?"My boss asked me the moment I entered into his cabin.

"Yes sir. Very much." I replied quite confidently.

"That's very good. Here is your ticket and visa. I wish you all the very best and hope that you would come out winner." He gave me an envelope and my passport which had come by than.

"I would be going to Delhi in an hour and thus decided to give your things as we would not be able to meet for some time." he continued.

"Wish you all the best." He said and we shook hands and came out of the cabin.

I came back to my cubical. Had a glass of cold water and started collecting important documents and paper that I had to take along with me. I kept on checking all the drawers for things which I had kept in the drawers over the years. I checked and rechecked all the documents and paper stuffed in the files and took whatever I felt important for me. While doing that I found the print out of the last mail that Pia had written to me while I was about to go for my placement interview. I had kept that mail with me and used to read it days after my interview and placement. I started reading it again when pundir came from behind. I hid the paper when I saw him standing over there.

"What are you hiding Mr London?" He asked me the moment he saw me hiding the paper.

"Hey, na..nothing. Just a letter from someone." I said in a hurry.

"Oho...letter from someone. May I know who is this someone?" He said quite cunningly.

"Cmon, its nothing. You tell me", I tried to avoid the topic.

"Well, today is your last day." He said quite melancholy.

"I would be really missing you."

"Hey you are saying as if I am going forever. I will be back in a year." I said.

"Yup, come to cafeteria around 2 PM. We have something special for you." He said and went towards his cubical.

I started reading the mail again.

There was a small get together at the cafeteria where people from my vertical had come to greet me. I met with everyone and took their permission to leave office early.

I do not know what had happened to me. The moment I came out of office and started to look for cab to go home, I felt like I should go to station one last time. Perhaps I would meet her today. I stopped there for a few minutes and started thinking which way I should move. Should I go to the station or moved towards home? My mind was saying that I should directly go home while heart was in favor of station. I was not able to decide what to do. I found myself helpless in front of heart and in a moment started to move towards the station. I took an auto rickshaw and told him to drop me at the VT station. I really do not know but my heart was saying that I would be able to meet her today. I entered into the station and as per my ritual for last three days sat on the same bench near the entrance of the platform from where she had taken the train that day. I sat there for a while and started looking at every other girl passing from there.

My eyes were searching her desperately. I sat there for an hour but did not find anyone remotely similar to her. I stood from there and went to take a cup of tea from nearby vendor. It was exactly six o'clock and while coming back to the bench from there, I saw someone from behind. I knew it was Pia. I saw her stepping towards the standing train and saw the time on the hanging clock over there. It was 6 pm BL local. I saw the time and moved my step faster. I saw train started to leave from the platform. I ran towards it. I didn't want to leave this train. I had to catch it at any cost. I threw my cup on the track and ran faster. The train had started to take speed and I was running like mad to catch it. I finally managed to take hold of the handle in front of the bogey and in a second jumped inside the train. Before I could realized, I saw hordes of women and girls inside the train and knew that I had entered into a girls bogey. I saw them staring to me like people stare at a stranger inside the house.

"I..I...I am sorry." I said hurriedly before I found myself in a mess.

"I am really sorry but I had to catch this train. I mean, I was looking for someone and I saw her enter into the bogey." I was hesitatingly saying.

"I mean......" Before I could speak I saw Pia from a distance.

She had not seen me.

I went towards her oblivious of the fact that i was in a girl compartment, in the middle of so many girls and soon be penalized for it.

"Hi Pia." I said very softly.

She was stunned.

The scene was like any bollywood movie.

For a minute she didn't utter a word. I didn't know so many eyes were staring at me. I found her a little unconscious.

"Where have you been for so many years dear." I said and she stood from the seat.

"Hey." She could only uttered and looked at everyone who by now had watching us like some shooting of bollywood movie is on.

"Hey, Rahul. You are here." I could see the uncomfortableness that she was feeling.

She could never imagine that we would ever meet like that.

It was really very embarrassing over there and thus we got down at the next station.

As we were coming out of the station I could see a strange reaction from her. It had never happened between us. I could sense the same attachment were not present. She kept looking down and walked out of the station with me. I did not know what to say. I had never imagined that we would be so uncomfortable to see each other.

She remained silent for a few moments before I broke the silent.

"How are you Dear? Where had you been? Why didn't you contact me even though you are here?"

I had so many questions to ask her.

She again remained silent for a second and said raising her head and looking at my eyes.

"It's all over Rahul."

I was stunned. I remain silent for a few minutes. I do not know what to do and kept on looking at her before she said again.

"I have been married to someone else Rahul. I could not keep the promise that I had given to you."

I was feeling like earth slipping down my feet and I was going deep inside it. It felt as if someone banged my head with something hard and I was praying for survival. In all these excitement I could not see a little sign of marriage over her forehead. I could not see the bangles and the mangalsutra that she was wearing. I didn't know how to react and thus I mumble an incoherent reply and just muttered,

"How has all this happened?"

"It does not matter now Rahul. I do not feel it would make any difference to our life. We have to accept that everything finished and we would move in our respective directions."

It was so easy to say all these things. She didn't know how much trouble I have faced.

"It didn't matter to you Pia but it really matters to me. I need to know why did you do this to me." I murmured.

"You will never imagine what have I suffered all these years without you Pia. I have missed you every moment of my life. You were in every breadth of mine. How could I forget you Pia. It would be very easy for you to forget me but how could I."

"I have waited for you all these years. I knew that one day you would come to me."

She didn't take it and I saw tears rolling down from her eyes.

I could still feel the love and care in her eyes. I wanted to know what had happened to her which resulted in her a drastic change. I could sense the difference in her. She didn't appear to be the one I had known for so many years. The excitement on her face had gone. She looked much older than her age. I could easily read the disappointment on her face. The disappointment of losing out on something.

What she narrated afterwards would echo in my brain forever. She had left for Mumbai the day we met for the last time. There had been some problem with her family. Her father had been charged with the contempt of court and thus had been put behind bars in Canada. He has been in a relationship with a Canadian woman for a year. The problem started when the woman conceived. Her father refused to accept the fact that he is the father of the child. The woman went to court for the paternity test and court had passed the order for a DNA test which her father had refused resulted in the contempt of court. There had been a number of quarrels between him and his brother when they had come to know about it. Her brother had almost distanced himself from the matter and had left contacting them. He hasd moved to UK and had settled over there. She wanted to protect the dignity of her family and thus had not told me at that time. She wanted that if things would improve then she would return to India. This didn't happen.

They moved to Canada in a week from Mumbai. She went from pillar to post to save her father from further embarrassment. She met with many lawyers and understood the law. She hired them and fought the case. Whatever savings her father was done had went into the legal battle.

The case went on for almost six months when her father was released from jail moreover with the pre condition that he has to marry the women or pay her million dollars as compensation within stipulated time. Her father didn't want to marry the woman and thus wanted to come out of this ignominious situation. She and her mother remained with him and wanted to come out of this situation.

They could not arrange such amount within the stipulated time and thus the woman moved to court again. There case had been going on for months and they had been losing whatever money they were having. The misfortune didn't end there. Her father got a severe heart attack and had to be shifted to a hospital. He could not withstand the pressure of court cases and most importantly facing his family after what had happened. She was the only one stood upfront in every difficulty. She had to look after her ailing father as well as the duo of sister and mother. The misery didn't seem to be end. He remained in hospital for a month. She fought the battle alone. The court case went on for another six months when finally they could come for an out of court settlement and agreed upon a figure which is significantly less than the original figure. They sold whatever properties they had in India and also borrowed from family and friends and finally able to pay the compensation. Within a month they flew back to India and moved to Mumbai at her maternal uncle place.

I stood silent there like a pole and looked at her eyes. The hordes of tears kept rolling down from them. I didn't speak a single word and kept looking at her. I could not imagine the suffering she had been undergone. Her father had been under medication since then. He could not recover from what had happened in Canada. For a few months they stayed in her maternal uncle house in Mumbai. She joined a company and started earning for the family. They sold their properties in Ranchi and finally settled in Mumbai. She had been taken the responsibilities of her family and worked day in and day out for the entire requirement to be fulfilled. Her sister restarted her school in Mumbai.

Whatever I was hearing was nerve racking and I could feel my skull breaking apart into millions pieces. The heart was thumping and the mind was numb. I thought I had lost speech. The world seemed to stand silent and I could hardly feel my frozen lips move. Her words kept echoing in my eardrums and producing a deafening sound, I had lost my ability to think. We stood silent for a few moments and looked at each other.

Almost incoherently I spoke to her when she stooped,

"You have suffered so much honey. Why didn't you tell me once, I would have come leaving behind everything for you dear."

"I was in danger Rahul. My family was in danger." She opened up a bit.

I could barely hear her already sinking voice. She could barely move her lips after that. I could feel the heaviness in her voice.

"Every time I was down and out, I used to remember you. I wanted to come back to you. It was all happening one after another and I just could not able to control things." She continued with broken voice.

"I always had you in my mind."

"I wanted to tell you everything. I wanted to tell you how much I needed you Rahul, but…." She stopped in the middle.

"But what dear, why didn't you asked me? You didn't trust me honey? You knew how much I love you and what you meant to me."

I asked holding both her hands.

"I stopped myself doing that. I knew how much have you worked for it. I know you were on the verge of achieving your much desire dream. I just could not think of spoiling all your efforts for me." She said.

"But this life of mine is because of you Pia. You have taught me how to live life. You have taught me how to fight. I owe a lot to you Pia for whatever I have achieved in my life.

You have not given me the opportunity to do something for you Pia. It could have been made a lot of difference. We could have been together."

"It was not meant to Rahul we were not destined to meet. It all happened so abruptly. I just couldn't think anything beyond saving my family from going into dumps. It was really scary."

I could understand the pain she had been undergone. The more I come to know the reality the more I had been falling in love with her. I had been so fortunate to have spent some memorable time with such a beautiful person on earth. My respect for her had increased many folds. When I see my suffering in absence of her, it looked absolutely negligible. She is the one who silently suffered everything and did not even let me know what had been undergoing. I have no grudges against her after what I had heard.

"But why didn't you call me or reach to me when you come back to Mumbai?" I had one more question to ask.

I did not plan anything Rahul. Faith had been planning everything and I was just following the instruction. We had already drained financially as well as mentally when we reached Mumbai.

We had none where we could have gone. It was all over for us. My father was not in a condition to resume any work. He had almost lost his consciousness. We stayed for a few months in my maternal uncle house. But you know it was so tough for them to adjust all of us in his already cramped house. They had been compromising on many things on our arrival." She continued for a few moments.

"Then,

One day they had been forced to tell us to find something for ourselves. I started looking for a house in Mumbai but after month of search could not get a decent place to leave and then one fine day while discussing it to my boss," and she stopped in between,

"What happened? Why did you stop?"

"My boss proposed me and asked me to marry him. He had been living in Mumbai with her mother and thus wanted to marry me. He said he always liked me and wanted to marry me and in return he would be keeping my family in his place and looked after them like a son."

"I thought about you Rahul. I did try to mail you and tell you that please come to me. But the same feeling of guilt had stopped me. It had been almost 2 years that we had met. I knew you must have been trying to establish your career. I didn't want to come back to your life and forced with all these things. I knew you had been trying to fulfill your dreams and I know what it means to me. I thought at least you live your life with the way you wanted."

I had seen relationship. My own brother had not come forward to take his responsibilities. I had to do something before it could go further down. I thought about the proposal and I thought about my family. I knew he is really caring for my family. He was really sweet to them and I knew it could save my family from a lot of trouble. I took this decision keeping all these in mind.

"And what about you Pia? Did you think about you?" I looked at her eyes and asked. Hey eyes were still wet.

"It does not matter now Rahul. I had already lost everything. At least my family is getting back to normal. My sister has resumed her study. He is really taking care of my family like a son"

It was already 8 pm and she wanted to return home.

"I should go now Rahul. They must have been looking for me." She said and tried to wipe her already dry eyes from her dupatta.

I could not stop her. She started to move towards the station and I kept on looking at her the same manner as she was going away from me the first time. Only difference was, this time I was very proud to see her going away from her. I was really proud that I had been loved by this beautiful creature. She would be in my mind and in my soul for the rest of my life. She had taught me a wonderful lesson. Life is not about living for oneself. I kept looking her until she disappeared from my eyes. I returned home that night and took my dad out for a scroll. I told him the entire story about the girl who had made his son whatever he is today. Next evening I boarded the British airways flight to Heathrow airport.

TEN YEARS LATER....

After what happened to him, Rishi left his study in the middle and went on to formed a nonprofit organization, GrowWell. The organization was private funded and the main objective was to provide a good life to poor kids. He had a tumultuous life and had seen lots of ups and down and thus wanted to assure that these kids do not fall victims and lead a normal life. They had been nurtured well and send to good school for formal education. From a small beginning, GrowWell has started to get recognition for the work it has been doing and had now receiving great amount of funds from the countries across the globe. I had last heard of him receiving a humanitarian award from a foreign body and thus am very happy for him. He met with a kind, sensitive and understanding woman along the way. They had the same passion of improving the condition of poor and needy. They fell in love and eventually married. They had a five years old son who is more inclined towards football and already won many medals at the school level.

Ruchika had left for the United States the day I had returned from London. We had a little interaction over the period of times. She and Rakesh had married against the wishes of their parents. They have settled in US for last five years and now have a three years old daughter.

When we last spoke she had been trying to send her daughter to a teen school in New York.

I have not heard of Ravi for last five years. In fact, none of us has any idea about his whereabouts. He never tried to contact us as well. He last called me five years ago when he had changed his job and was about to move to Mumbai to join a bank. Knowing him well, I am sure that he would have been doing great for himself wherever and whatever he would be doing.

Priyesh did his MBA in grand style and had joined a tea manufacturing company in Darjeeling.

He worked there for two years and left to join an entrepreneurial course in United States. He went on to form a tea processing company in Kolkata and doing a great job. He did not join his family business. He is married to a Bengali girl and has a 3 years old daughter.

Asad has not returned from Dubai and is settled there. He has been working with a FMCG company and looking after international marketing. He keeps on visiting many countries and shares his experience over phone. Sometime, we discussed about the past when we did not know if we ever come out of this small city and make our life. Today he has been crossing miles across continents and thus is very proud of himself. He is married and has two cherubic sons.

Life has changed for good for Namit. He could not come out of his hometown after the demise of his father. He had to look after his mother and his family. He did try in a few companies but did not really like to continue in day to day job. He faced some kinds of

financial burden initially but pulled it right at the end. He opened one electronics appliances store in Ranchi and has been exclusive dealers for a number of big brands. A very strange thing happened to his life. He got to meet Ria's sister one fine day at the shop. They clicked immediately and now are married and have a two years old son.

Shreya tried one more time to convince me a life away from Pia. I really respect and admire her feelings and thought very hard to think of a life without Pia but could not manage. She went to United Kingdom and done masters in journalism. We have not been in touch since and what I come to know she has been married to an NRI and has been working with a foremost broadcasting company in UK.

After returning from London, I resumed my responsibilities in Mumbai. I did not meet Pia after that night. I started concentrating on my job and keep on moving from one place to another. I had been getting recognition for my work and now heading one of the bestselling brands in the company. I did not find anyone else who could replace Pia from my heart and keep on moving in life with the shadow of the girl I loved the most.